AN EYE FOR AN EYE
Kent Conwell

For twelve years, four months, and six days, Jed Walker doggedly clung to one goal: kill the five owlhoots who had shot him and murdered his brother.

Only after he was nursed back to health after a second ambush did he begin to realize that his hate-filled mission came at an expensive price, years wasted from his own life.

Then, after all that time, the trail grew hot. Jed pursues two of the remaining three killers through Southeast Texas to Sabinetown where he learns the identity of the third man. The third man turns out to be the one who not only nursed him back to health, but became his friend in the meantime.

In anguish, Jed Walker stands at the crossroads of his life. How can he kill the man who saved his life?

Other books by Kent Conwell:

AN EYE
FOR
AN EYE

•

Kent Conwell

AVALON BOOKS
NEW YORK

© Copyright 2004 by Kent Conwell
Library of Congress Catalog Card Number: 2003095462
ISBN 0-8034-9640-0
Published by Thomas Bouregy & Co., Inc.
160 Madison Avenue, New York, NY 10016

PRINTED IN THE UNITED STATES OF AMERICA
ON ACID-FREE PAPER
BY HADDON CRAFTSMEN, BLOOMSBURG, PENNSYLVANIA

To Jessica. Thanks for your friendship.
And to my wife, Gayle, who is always there for me.

Chapter One

Somewhere in the Old Testament, it reads "An eye for an eye, a tooth for a tooth." That's what I was taught, but as I grew older, the rules that were once so clear and exact slowly grew muddled and confusing. More than once, during and after the War of Oppression, I longed for my earlier years when right was right and wrong was wrong.

Despite the passing of those simple days, the one unwavering conviction I clung to was that I had to keep going until I ran down the vermin who had ambushed me and my brother. They left us both for dead. I survived, but William, my older brother, didn't make it.

The norther swept across the Red River and slammed into East Texas with an icy blast of sleet that froze the very marrow in a jasper's bones. I was an expert on weather, for I'd been through storms in Montana and Illinois that didn't begin to drive the chill as deep into an hombre's body as those Texas northers.

That was the sorry state of the weather when I rode into Nacogdoches and put my pony in the livery. Shivering in my boots and ducking my head into the sleet, I slogged my way across the streets of ankle-deep mud to the nearest saloon and bellied up to the bar. A dozen or so jaspers sat scattered among several tables while a handful stood around the cherry-red, pot-bellied stove in the middle of the room.

I'd been in hundreds of saloons like this one, hundreds more that were mere shacks, and hundreds that were nothing more than holes dug in the side of a hill. Truth was, I'd lost count of the number of saloons I'd gone into over the last twelve years in search of the remaining three owlhoots who killed my brother.

I paid for the drink of cheap whiskey and woodenly asked the same question I'd asked a thousand times before. "I'm looking for an hombre. Medium sized." I drew my fingers across the bridge of my nose and down my cheek. "Got a scar here."

The bartender paused in wiping down the bar, then shook his head. "Don't remember nobody like that. Sorry, pard."

A few feet down the bar, a thin cowpoke wearing a black slicker and rain-sodden hat glanced at me, then quickly shifted his gaze back to the mug of beer before him. I couldn't help noticing he was missing the little finger on his left hand. Otherwise, I didn't give him another thought. I downed my drink and headed for the next saloon. I had no idea how many saloons were in Nacogdoches, but before the night was finished, I would hit each one and ask the same question.

As usual, I came up empty. As usual, I bowed my neck and swore to keep looking.

During the night, the sleet turned to rain. Come morning, the chilling north wind continued whipping through the tall pines, numbing any flesh exposed to it. Reluctantly, I climbed out of my soogan, which I had spread in the stall with my dun pony.

Ten minutes later, I rode out, heading for the next town down the narrow trace winding through the tall pines.

An hour down the road, I was shot out of my saddle.

The last thought I had as I slammed into the cold mud was what a blasted trick God had played on me. Now I would never be able to avenge the death of my brother.

The next thing I remember was the steady, mesmerizing patter of drizzle on the wood shake roof over my head. How long I lay just listening, I don't know. Finally, beneath the patter of rain, I picked up the crackling of burning wood, and then I smelled the pungent aroma of wood smoke.

I turned my head on the pillow and stared at a blazing fire that cast dancing shadows about the dark room. A dull throb pulsed in my head. The only thought I could pull clear of the jumble in my brain was that I was alone.

Exhausted by my few moments of consciousness, I slipped back into a healing slumber.

Next time I awakened, sunlight filled the room. The rain had ceased, but the fire still blazed. A slight woman was bending over the hearth, stirring a small pot at the edge of the coals. A rich, savory aroma assailed my nostrils. My stomach growled.

I shifted around on the bunk. The ticking in the mattress crackled.

The slight woman glanced over her shoulder. A smile played over her heart-shaped face. "Well, see you finally decided to wake up." She tapped the spoon against the pot a few times to rid it of the excess stew. As she busily poured water into a washbowl and rinsed out a washrag, she continued talking. "My name's Mary Catherine Hopkins. My brother, Arch, found you on the road a couple days back."

She continued her explanation while she knelt by the bunk and gently washed my face, taking care with my forehead. "You were lucky. The slug bounced off your head. Cut a nasty gash, but it didn't appear to crack anything." She sat back on her heels. "No infection. Another day or so, you'll be fine. Does it hurt much?"

Before, I'd been too numb to feel much, but now I

could feel the pounding—a pounding mighty close to what I experienced the times when I'd had too much of that old Monongahela whiskey. I squeezed my eyes shut. "Some," I mumbled. "Some."

"Well," she said, her tone full of authority. "Soon as we get some beef stew down you, it'll start feeling much better." Gently, she raised my head and slipped another pillow behind me. I couldn't help noticing just how fresh and clean she smelled.

With quick, sure movements, she reached for a bowl on the hearth. "You're bound to be hungry," she said, turning back to the pot and scooping up several spoonfuls of steaming stew.

Sitting down on the edge of my bunk, she started to feed me like I was a baby.

Despite the pounding in my head, the stew was the most delicious I had ever tasted. In my years, I'd lined up at many a chuckwagon, bellied up to many a bar, and scooted under many a café table, but I couldn't remember a time when any grub could begin to compare with her steaming stew.

I was ready for a second bowl, but Mary Catherine held a tin cup of cold water to my lips. "That's enough for now. You rest. When you wake up next time, you can have more."

She slipped the pillow from under my head and rose to her feet. "I'll be right here when you awaken." Her dark brown eyes smiled at me.

I started to protest, but a feeling of warmth and

comfort enveloped me. Before I could even mumble a thank-you, I was asleep.

From somewhere in the far recesses of my slumber, I heard the rain begin once again, this time with a sharper beat. From time to time, voices overpowered the rain. Then, slowly, the noises grew more and more distant.

Next time I awakened, I saw Mary Catherine and a jasper about my age sitting at the table around a glowing a coal oil lamp. They spoke in muted tones.

Mary Catherine leaned forward. "Did you find out who he is, Arch?"

Arch pulled a bag of Bull Durham from his leather vest, which was studded with silver dollar conchos. "I looked through his plunder. He's poorer than Job's turkey."

"But what about his name? Anything there saying who he is?"

He gave his head a half shake and touched a match to his cigarette. "Under the saddle fender was the name J. S. Walker. I reckon that's who he is, unless he stole the rig."

The young woman shook her head. "He doesn't look like a horse thief to me."

Arch laughed. "I swan, sis. You never think bad of no one."

Playfully, she slapped at him and bounced to her feet. "You'd be better off if you did the same. Now, you go out and bring us another bucket of water while

I tend to our supper. Bring it into the kitchen, then come back in here and watch after Mister Walker."

"Yes, ma'am," Arch replied, laughing and donning his slicker.

Mary Catherine opened the door and stepped onto a porch. Across the porch was another door that opened into a brightly lit room. Arch followed her out, closing the door behind him.

I lay silent, motionless, staring at the leaping flames in the rock fireplace. I wondered just who these folks were.

A few minutes later, Arch came back in, shucking his slicker and shaking the raindrops onto the wood plank floor. He stopped when he spotted me watching him. "Hey, partner. You're awake. How you feeling?"

"Tolerable," I mumbled. "Much obliged to you folks."

Arch laughed. "You is mighty lucky to be able to feel tolerable, my friend." While he spoke, he pulled a coffeepot from the coals and poured a cup. "That slug took a hunk out of your skull. You'll always have a dent up there. A little bit more, and you'd be out on the trail looking for a chunk of your noggin. Here you go. Sip this," he added, handing me the coffee.

Scooting up in the bunk so I could lean against the wall, I fought back the dizziness threatening me. "Thanks." I grimaced at the throbbing in my head. "My Pa always said I had a hard head."

Arch slid a chair beside the bunk and straddled it

backwards so he could rest his arms on the back of the chair. "Reckon he was right."

The coffee was just what I needed, six-shooter coffee so thick that it jelled when it cooled off. "Good belly wash," I said, nodding appreciatively.

I was feeling better, some dizzy, but stronger. I noticed I was wearing strange long johns. I held up one arm to Arch. "These ain't mine."

He grinned. It was a friendly, warm smile. "They're mine. You was soaked through and through. Probably caught your death if we'd left you in them wet clothes."

My eyes grew wide, and I looked at the closed door.

He laughed again. "Don't worry none, partner. Sis helped me get you in here, but I changed you myself. She's done all the looking after since. Why, she looks after you better than she does our old tabby cats."

I sipped the coffee again. "Well, I'm much obliged." I paused, then added. "Arch? That's your name?"

His grin broadened. "Arch for short. Real name is Archibald. Archibald Samuel Hopkins. You see why folks just call me Arch?"

At that moment, the slab door swung open and Mary Catherine stepped inside. When she spotted me sitting up, she jerked to a halt and smiled. "Well, you look better than you did this morning."

"I feel a heap more spry, ma'am," I replied. "A heap."

She glanced at Arch. "Supper's ready. Pa'll be in directly. I'll bring some in to our guest."

I took another sip of coffee. "If you don't mind, I think I can make it to the kitchen table."

Arch and Mary Catherine exchanged a look of uncertainty. Arch shrugged. "Sure. I'll get you some duds. Your boots are dry, I reckon, but they'll be a little stiff."

"Thanks."

He hesitated. "I cleaned the knife you carry in the right boot. Never known a man to carry a knife in his boot."

I glanced at Mary Catherine. "Comes in handy at times," I replied.

He shrugged and waved his sister out. "Give us some privacy, sis. The man wants to get dressed."

With an embarrassed smile, she stepped out the door and closed it behind her. While rummaging through a hand-hewn chest, Arch asked, "What's your handle, partner?"

"Walker," I replied. "Jed Walker."

He grunted and handed me a stack of clothes. "Reckon these will fit you, Jed. We're about the same size."

"Thanks."

"Where was you heading?"

I looked up. "When?"

"When you was bushwhacked. Where were you bound?"

I hesitated, then fixed him with an icy stare. "To kill three men."

Chapter Two

I managed to slip into my dry duds and stomp into my boots without falling over on my side. My head still pounded, and from time to time I had to steady myself, but soon I was dressed. With Arch's help, I made it across the dogtrot into the kitchen.

On the stove was a platter heaped with steaks, a pot of simmering beans, a bowl brim-full of red-eye gravy, a spider of potatoes, a pan of golden brown biscuits, and a pot of steaming coffee.

Half a dozen wranglers were lined up by the stove, waiting. I didn't know for what, but I didn't have long to find out. A few moments later, a ramrod-straight old jasper who looked like he was made of iron ingots pushed through the door and tossed his hat on a peg.

"That's Pa," Arch whispered. "We don't start without him."

I could see why.

Like a king, Stillman Hickory Hopkins picked up a tin plate, went to the head of the line, filled it full, and poured his coffee. Then he took his place at the head of a ten-foot sawbuck table.

The others followed suit, seating themselves around the table.

No one ate.

Mary Catherine waited until Arch and me served and seated ourselves before she filled her plate and took her place at the opposite end of the table from her pa.

Stillman bowed his head. "Bless this grub, Lord. Keep the Comanche away. Help the grass grow. Amen."

I discovered quickly that Stillman and his brood, hands and all, believed that meals were for eating and not talking. Scarce a word other than "pass this" or "pass that" was uttered.

I took this as a chance to study my new acquaintances. Mary Catherine was slender, with dark eyes and dark hair. Her bright smile stood out in sharp contrast against her dark complexion. Arch was her all over again, except about my size and naturally more rugged. The wranglers, Speck, Bones, Cranky, and several others, were typical rail-thin, weather-beaten cowpokes. The one they called Red, who was about a head taller than me, sat next to Mary Catherine. I had the feeling he wanted everyone to think he owned her.

One thing I had to admit, the old man had everyone

trained. As they finished, they dropped their dishes in the boiling water in the wreck pan on the stove, then retired to the bunkhouse for a smoke and a friendly game of poker.

Stillman, Arch, Red, and me remained at the table while Mary Catherine tidied up the kitchen. The old man packed his pipe, and, while lighting it, asked, "Where you from, boy?"

I shrugged. "All over, Mister Hopkins."

Red spoke up, a trace of sarcasm in his voice. "Driftin', huh?"

I glanced sidelong at Mary Catherine, who was washing the dishes. For some strange reason, I didn't want her to think I was just a no-account drifter. "Some. Just seeing the country."

Arch frowned at me. I felt a tinge of guilt, at the same time wishing I had said nothing about wanting to kill three men. "That's not exactly true, Mister Hopkins. I don't want to lie to you folks. You helped me out. Saved my life. Truth is, I'm looking for the men who killed my brother."

Stillman's eyes cut toward Arch, then swept back to me, studying me closely. He nodded briefly. "How long you been looking?"

"Before the war. Twelve years. Twelve years, four months, and if today is the thirteenth, six days."

The old man puffed his pipe and shook his head. "That's a mighty big chunk out of your life just looking for revenge."

"Reckon you're right. But I'll go another twelve if I got to."

He studied me a moment longer. "I think you would, son. Well, good luck to you. You're welcome to stay on here as long as you want."

Mary Catherine smiled at me, and Arch nodded his head.

"Thanks, but as soon as I'm able, I'll ride out."

Stillman grunted. "Your choice."

Later, as Arch and I got ready for bed, I asked him about Red. "Seems awful possessive of your sister."

Arch laughed. "Yeah. His name is Lew Buchanan. You can see from his hair why we call him Red. His pa owns the Circle B next to us. He figures he's got Sis roped and hogtied, but I tell you, there ain't no one who'll hogtie her if she don't want to be hogtied."

I chuckled and climbed into bed. *Mary Catherine.* That was a pleasant thought, but I put it out of my mind. Even if I did have the time, I didn't reckon I was good enough to ever get into the same room with her.

The weather cleared. As is typical of the fickle Texas winter, three or four days of spring-like weather followed. The wound on my head scabbed over. I grew stronger each day, and within a week, I was ready to grab the bit in my teeth and pull foot out of there.

Still, I continued to puzzle over who had ambushed me. Right away, I discounted highwaymen. I had little that was valuable, and when Arch found me, I still had it. My pony had been grazing not far from where I lay, so that ruled out horse thieves.

That left the townspeople.

I'd caused no trouble in Nacogdoches, spoken only to bartenders, didn't play any poker, and certainly didn't insult any saloon girls.

While the theory was a stretch of the imagination, the only explanation that made any sense was that someone must have learned I was looking for the hombre with the scar. If that was true, then that meant I was closing in on my quarry.

I decided to ride back into Nacogdoches and question the bartenders again, this time as to whether anyone had questioned them about me.

My dun was rested and eager to run. Arch looked on in the barn as I adjusted my sixgun on my hip and tied my Mackinaw behind the candle with my soogan. "You sure you don't want me to ride in with you, Jed? It's about ten, twelve miles."

I swung into the saddle. "Appreciate the thought, but I can do this myself." I leaned over and offered my hand. "Thanks for all the help."

He frowned. "You ain't coming back?"

"If I find something, I'm following it."

He nodded and glanced at the house. "You ought to tell Mary Catherine good-bye."

My ears burned. I shrugged. "I—ah, well, I don't reckon I'm much good at saying good-bye. You tell her for me."

He nodded. "I will. And don't forget, you don't learn nothing, come on back. You hear?"

I winked at him. "I'll do that."

Strangely enough, I hated to leave the Bar H. The feeling of being around a real family was mighty comforting.

An hour or so out from the Bar H, I ran across a heap of horse sign—shod and unshod ponies. I studied the tracks. Best I could figure were eight, maybe ten horses. Resting my hands on the saddle horn, I leaned forward and peered to the west. "Were it a couple months later, boy," I said to my dun pony, "I'd figure Comanche, but not now, not in the middle of winter. They'll be holed up somewhere, all nice and warm." With a click of my tongue, I urged my pony into a running walk. "Probably some wranglers pushing a few strays back home," I muttered.

At the third saloon in Nacogdoches, I got lucky. "Yeah, I remember you," said the bartender, an amiable gent with mutton chop whiskers. "You was looking for some jasper—had a scar, I think." He slid my whiskey down the bar.

"That's me. Got another question. After I left, did anyone come in asking about me?" I sipped my whiskey.

Without hesitation, he replied. "Sure did. Couldn't help remembering. Reason is, it seemed odd one should come in looking for some jasper and then later, another jasper come in looking for the first."

"You remember what he looked like?" I forced a grin.

He wiped at the bar. "Sure do. Small man. Wore a black slicker and a hat sagging down over his ears." He paused. "He a friend of yours?"

A black slicker. I remembered the small hombre who stood at the bar with me at the saloon my first night in town. With an indifferent shrug, I replied, "We know each other. You could say I'm in debt to him, and I'd certainly like to give him what he's got coming. He still in town?"

"Ain't seen him since. That don't mean he left town."

I downed the remainder of my whiskey. "Obliged."

Figuring that if the hombre was still in town, he'd have his horse at one of the liveries, I started making the rounds. Ten minutes later, on the north side of the square at Barnes' Livery, I stood fidgeting while a wizened old man settled a chaw of tobacco in his cheek. "Yep. Remember him. Bone thin. Rode in one morning."

"When was this? You remember?"

He frowned as he concentrated, at the same time working on the chaw in his mouth. "Maybe a week or so back. Around time the last storm. Hung around a few days, then pulled out."

"He say where he was heading?"

The old man squirted a brown stream of tobacco

juice onto the straw-strewn ground and switched the wad to his other cheek. "Naw, but I watched from the door when he pulled out. He headed north."

My hopes soared. I had never before been so close to one of the gang that shot my brother down. I struggled to keep my voice calm. "North, huh? What was he riding?"

"Purty animal. Strawberry roan. Tall one. About fifteen, maybe sixteen hands. Don't see too many of them around. Why, I remember the last . . ."

I paid no attention to his recollections. He had given me all the information I needed. I nodded. "Obliged."

As I left the livery, I spotted a cowpoke pulling up at the sheriff's office. What really caught my attention was the horse he was leading, a strawberry roan.

A feeling of dread swept over me. For the first time in years, I was close to the ones I sought. I muttered a fast prayer that nothing had gone wrong.

Sporting a week-old beard, the gaunt cowpoke was standing in front of the sheriff's desk when I walked in. Both men looked around. "Hold your horses, cowboy. I'll get to you in a minute," said the sheriff.

I stepped up to the desk. "If you don't mind, Sheriff, I'm interested in what this jasper here has to say about that strawberry roan outside."

Both men frowned.

I explained. "I'm looking for the cowboy who rode out of town on that roan."

The gaunt cowpoke grunted. "He a friend of yours, cowboy?"

"Nope. Truth be, I never met him, but if he's who I think, he can answer a heap of questions for me."

With a brief shake of his head, the cowpoke hooked his thumb at the sheriff and replied. "I reckon you're out of luck, friend. Like I was telling Sheriff Bonner here, the Comanche kilt the old boy who was forking that roan. I run across him about twenty miles or so north of here on the old Spanish trail to Natchitoches. They cut him up something fierce. Skinned his face."

"Did you happen to notice if he was missing the little finger on his left hand?"

He shook his head. "Told you he was cut up. They chopped off his hands and feet. Nothing left but stumps."

I grimaced. Maybe at least I could get a name. "He have anything on him that might say who he was?"

"Nope." With a laconic drawl, he added, "Stripped the old boy clean. Took everything."

I glanced at the strawberry roan standing hipshot at the rail. "Wonder why the Comanche didn't take him? They got good eyes for a sound pony."

The sheriff spoke up. "Who can say? Could be the pony spooked off into the woods and come back later." He eyed me suspiciously. "What was that jasper to you?"

I slid my hat back and pointed to the two-inch-long scab on my forehead. "I got me a hunch him or one of his partners gave me this."

Sheriff Bonner's eyes narrowed. "What's your name, cowboy?"

"Walker. Jed Walker. Arch Hopkins found me alongside the trace last week. Him and his family nursed me back. I rode out this morning to see if I could find who bushwhacked me."

The Sheriff nodded slowly, studying me. His eyes grew hard. "Well, I never cottoned to backshooters none, but I ain't putting up with no trouble in my town. Start it up, and I'll toss that lanky behind of yours in one of my cells."

I chuckled. "Sheriff, you got nothing to worry about. But I promise you, if I decide to stir up trouble, I'll tell you first."

"Fair enough. Now—"

The door slammed open. Freckle-faced Speck burst in, shouting, "Sheriff! Come quick. The Comanche hit the Bar H! Stole the horses and shot up the place. The old man is hurt terrible bad."

Chapter Three

A Comanche arrow had struck Stillman Hopkins in the back and come out through his chest. Mary Catherine had cut off the flinthead, tied a coal oil-soaked rag to the arrow, and pulled it back through his chest. Then she washed the holes out with whiskey.

Despite the wound, the old man refused to take to bed. "They hit this morning," he said. "Them blasted heathens." He fired a blistering look at Arch. "Well, boy. You going after them, or you plan on sitting around here all day?"

Arch looked up from packing his saddlebags. "Just hold your horses, Pa. We'll get them back." He ordered two of his wranglers to remain behind. "I don't reckon on no more trouble, but I'll feel better if someone's around here to look after the old man."

Stillman exploded. " 'The old man!' Why, you wet-behind-the-ears little—"

Arch laughed. "I figured that would get your dander up. You just keep it up while we're gone." He glanced at me. "Didn't find what you was looking for, huh?"

"Nope. Comanches got the old boy. Butchered him up something terrible." I glanced at Mary Catherine, who had a right attractive smudge of gunpowder on her button nose, then back to Arch. "Give me a fresh horse, and I'll ride with you."

He grinned. "I was hoping you would." His grin faded. "You sure you feel like it?"

I patted my forehead. "If somebody wants to get rid of me, they best shoot me somewhere else besides the head."

He nodded to the corral. "Take that sorrel. He's got staying power."

With Sheriff Bonner leading the way, we set out after the Comanche. The trail led west, toward open country. The Comanche were clever. They knew push-ing over a hundred head of horses through the pine forests meant certain capture. Instead, they headed for the prairies, where they kept the herd moving at a steady gait. I did some fast figuring, coming up with the notion that they were about twenty or so miles ahead of us.

There were eight of us. We rode fresh horses, plan-ning on pushing them hard for the first hour or so, then dropping back to a steady lope. I couldn't help noticing Red had not shown up to join the posse.

I don't know about the others, but I figured they were all as jittery as I was. I knew that for a fact when Speck called out from the back of our small party, "Just don't get in my way, boys. I feel like a good fight coming on."

Arch called over his shoulder. "Don't worry, Speck. First Comanche I see, I'll send him directly back to you."

"You do that, partner. You just do that. Me and Cranky'll do all the work, and you old boys just stand and watch."

Cranky grunted. "Don't go committing me to nothing."

We all laughed to keep up our courage.

Just before dark, the trail cut back north. The sheriff didn't let up. He stayed on the trail. As long as we were on the prairie, we could keep tracking in the starlight. A hundred sets of hooves tears up the ground worse than hogs rooting in a turnip patch.

Around ten or so, we pulled up. Sheriff Bonner called out. "Okay, boys. Take a break. Moon'll be up in an hour or two. Grab some sleep. We'll try to catch up with them heathens tonight."

Speck whistled. "If they don't get us first," he said, laughing.

We camped cold, taking care to picket our animals next to where we had tossed our soogans. After watering and graining our ponies, we sprawled on our blankets and dug out a supper of cold biscuit and fried venison.

Despite the unseasonably warm days, the winter nights cooled down quickly, so I sat cross-legged on my soogan with a blanket over my shoulders while I gnawed on my vittles.

Arch tore off a chunk of venison. "So you couldn't find the old boy you was after, huh?"

I shook my head. "Well, yes and no."

He snorted. "Sounds like the kind of answer I get from Mary Catherine sometimes."

I chuckled and told him what had taken place. "Just my luck. Closer than I ever been before."

Arch's face was hidden in the shadow cast by the brim of his Stetson. "How do you know this was one of them you're looking for?"

"Truth is," I replied, trying to answer the same question for my own benefit. "I'm not sure. Someone for a fact ambushed me. Now, I didn't cause no trouble in Nacogdoches, so it can't be someone out to get even. He didn't take anything, so it can't be robbery. I figure it had to be someone who heard me describing one of the owlhoots I'm after." I drew my finger across the bridge of my nose. "The one with the scar that runs over the nose and across the cheek."

Arch sat up straighter and cleared his throat. His face was still hidden in the shadow cast by his Stetson. "A scar? What kind of scar?" His voice seemed strained.

Over the years, I had replayed the image of that scar

49693

over and over in my head. "It's been a long time. Almost twelve years, but as I remember, it looks like the kind a jasper would get from a knife fight."

Speck interrupted. "Knife fight? I hear someone talking about a knife fight? Why, did I ever you tell you hombres about the big knife fight over in Fort Worth?" Without giving anyone a chance to answer, he continued. "There was this fancy cock-of-the-walk who sauntered into the White Elephant Saloon and started pushing a scrawny little feller around. Well, this little feller whips out a Bowie knife bigger'n him and promptly slices the big boy up. That's when some of the big boy's partners jumped in, and then some of the little feller's friends. Why, it was nothing but slashing knives and blood all over."

Speck rambled for another five minutes, regaling us with all the gory details and the final culmination of the donnybrook.

Later, as we lay in our soogans, Arch whispered. "Jed? You asleep?"

"Naw. What's wrong?"

"Ain't nothing. Just wondering. Whereabouts you from? Why was you after that feller? It have to do with them three men you said you had to kill?"

I remained silent for several seconds, long enough that Arch whispered, "I don't mean to butt in. You don't got to tell me nothing if you don't want."

For twelve years, counting the five in the war, I'd never confided my feelings to anyone. At first, rage drove me, a blinding, fire-breathing rage. Over the years, the heated passion of my fury cooled into an even more consuming cauldron of bubbling lava. Somehow, I felt that revealing my inner feelings, the truth, would be an act of disloyalty to my dead brother.

"It isn't that, Arch," I whispered, turning on my back and staring into the starry heavens. "I got some debts to settle for my brother. I appreciate you asking, but I don't know exactly how to explain it. I suppose it sounds foolish, but William and me was close, real close. We shared just about everything, even the whippings Pa handed out. I reckon what I'm going to do is the last thing I'll ever be able to share with my brother." I cleared my throat. "Like I said, it might sound foolish, but that's how it is, just between my brother and me."

Arch remained silent several seconds. His voice was soft and thin when he replied, "No. That don't sound foolish one bit. Not one bit. Just you remember, Jed. You decide you need any help, I'll be there for you."

That same feeling of warmth and comfort that had come over me that first day at the Bar H when Mary Catherine straightened my pillow came back over me. "Thanks, Arch."

We broke camp just after midnight as the waning moon rose over the tall pines to the east. The soft prairie soil, torn by the hooves of the herd we were following, muffled our passing. The only sounds were the squeak of leather, the jangle of O-rings, and the soft grunts of our ponies.

Two hours later, Sheriff Bonner pulled up. We gathered around him. He gestured to the broad, dark trail that angled northeast. "I was afraid of that."

Arch muttered a curse.

I spoke up. "What's going on?"

"The trail is leading directly to Lazenby Valley."

Several of the posse muttered.

"So?"

Sheriff Bonner scooted around in his saddle and looked at me. "So, Mister Walker, Lazenby Valley here is full of enough timbered ridges to hide a thousand Comanches. We ride down there, and we can count on an ambush."

With a shake of my head, I replied, "Well now, Sheriff, I'm not any too partial to an ambush, so I reckon we best take steps to avoid one." I studied the sprawling valley before us. It dropped away at least a couple hundred feet below us and spread a mile to either side. Despite the bluish glow of the waning moon, the far side of the valley was lost in the shadows.

"And how do you reckon on doing that, Mister Walker?"

I glanced at Arch and the cowpokes around him. "I'll listen to what any of you old boys have to say. You know this country, and I don't, but I've been around Indians from Missouri to Montana and out to Arizona. I've got no problem trying to sneak up on them while they sleep. Give me one man and I'll scout ahead."

Two or three of the cowpokes muttered their misgivings. Before Sheriff Bonner could reply, Arch spoke up. "I'll go."

"You sure, Arch?" It was Speck.

"Sure. Just a little walk in the dark."

I looked at the sheriff. "We'll ride in about a mile. If it's clear, we'll come back. Take some time, but that way we can ease across the valley."

Suddenly a match flared. Arch snapped, "Get rid of that match, Cranky. You don't need no cigarette right now."

Chagrined, Cranky mumbled, "Sorry, Arch. I wasn't thinking."

Sheriff Bonner growled, "Well, I reckon you best start then, don't you?"

I looked at Arch. "You ready?"

He pulled up beside me, he yanked off his Stetson, and dragged his arm across his forehead. "You don't have to do this, Jed. Them horses ain't yours. You stay here."

His face was taut with fear. I supposed mine was also. "Naw. I just feel like a stroll in the dark."

The gullies between the ridges below looked like bowls of black ink. We descended slowly into the first one. I was wound up tighter than a hangman's knot.

Chapter Four

Eyes nervously quartering the shadows around us, we shucked our sixguns and followed the broad trail down the gradual slope toward the first of the pine-covered ridges. The farther we rode, the tighter my muscles grew. I had to force myself to breathe, to relax.

The trail led between two rounded ridges that appeared to be about thirty or forty feet high. Underbrush lined the base of the ridges, and tall pines covered the sides and crests, reaching another hundred feet into the sky.

Arch leaned toward me and whispered. "You watch your side. I'll watch mine."

I nodded. My throat was so dry I couldn't have replied even if I wanted to.

There was little vegetation beneath the towering

pines, as the tall trees blocked the sunlight essential for growth. That worked to our advantage; the moonlight beyond the ridge sharply silhouetted the pines, offering a clear backdrop to spot any movement.

In the distance an owl hooted, answered within seconds by another. "Indians?" Arch whispered.

"Owls," I managed to croak out.

"Huh?"

"Mating."

"Oh."

Slowly, we followed trail. I dragged my tongue over my lips and tried to work up enough saliva to wet my dry throat. Suddenly, a crash in the vegetation at the base of the ridge startled us. As one, we jerked our revolvers up just as a deer halted in the middle of the trail. It stared at us for a few seconds before bolting up the adjoining ridge.

Arch blew softly through his lips. "I think I just aged ten years."

I tried to laugh. "Me too."

For the next ten minutes, we pushed deeper and deeper into the valley, every muscle in our bodies taut with fear. Finally I reined up. "Go back and get the others. I'll wait here. Anything goes wrong, I'll fire two shots."

With a terse nod, Arch wheeled his pony around and raced back up the trail, leaving me all by my lonesome in the middle of what seemed to be the darkest forest on the darkest night of my life.

I kept my eyes moving, studying the ridges ahead,

trying to put myself in the Comanches' head. The Comanche were excellent horsemen and gallant warriors.
But, like many other tribes, they had few leaders who
knew any fighting or any strategy other than sneak
attacks and frontal charges. I hoped the leader of this
raiding party was not one of those few.

I studied my surroundings. My guess was that if
they planned to ambush us, it would be from the ridges
as we passed beneath. Maybe they wouldn't be expecting us on the ridge, which was where I led the
posse when they returned with Arch.

"Makes sense," Sheriff Bonner whispered after I explained my reasoning.

"Up here, we're not wide open like down on the
trail. I got a feeling the Comanche won't be looking
for us on the ridges."

We rode in silence, winding our way through the
pines, trying to avoid the patches of moonlight. Sometime later, Speck muttered, "What if there ain't no
ambush? What if the Comanche just kept riding?"

"They didn't," the sheriff replied. "The Comanche'll settle down at night. I fought them along the
Brazos and Nueces before the war. Don't reckon
they've changed too much."

I drawled. "No disrespect intended, Sheriff, but I
hope you won't be offended if I don't count on that."

He chuckled. "Don't worry, Mister Walker. I ain't
going to count on it either."

Thirty minutes later, we smelled wood smoke.

"Hold it," Sheriff Bonner whispered. "They're up ahead."

The tang of wood smoke was light in the air, a fugitive drift on the light breeze.

The sheriff whispered his orders. "We'll go ahead on foot. Cranky, you stay with the horses. You others, grab your saddle guns and follow me."

I shucked my rifle, a Yellowboy Henry. I bought it just before enlisting in the Missouri Confederate Militia in 1862. It had a 15-shot magazine, which, along with my Colt handgun, gave me 20 shots—21 if I decided to load the sixth cartridge in the Colt cylinder.

Without a word, Sheriff Bonner led out, taking us on a serpentine course to avoid the shafts of moonlight striking the ground. I stayed right behind him, and the others strung out behind us. The ground was covered with a thick layer of pine needles, effectively muffling the sound of our feet.

The odor of wood smoke grew stronger. The sheriff looked at me, arching an eyebrow. I nodded.

From time to time, I glanced over my shoulder, beginning to grow uncomfortable with such a great distance between us and our ponies. I cursed myself for not telling Cranky that if he didn't hear from us in ten or fifteen minutes to move the horses forward.

Fifteen minutes later, the sheriff threw up his hand and dropped to one knee. We followed his lead. In the distance, a fire winked at us between the straight trunks of the tall pines.

He glanced over his shoulder. "Stay here. I'll see what's up ahead."

The others nodded, but I tagged right after him. He dropped a knee and growled, "I say, stay there."

I couldn't see his face in the darkness, nor he mine. The tone of my voice relayed my resolve. "Forget it, Sheriff. If I'm going to get into trouble, I want to see it for myself." Rising into a crouch, I moved past him. "If you're coming, come on. And stay out of the moonlight."

He muttered a curse but hurried to my side.

We remained on the crest of the ridge. As we drew closer to the fire, I laid a hand on his arm and pointed to the fire. I held up my rifle, then gestured to the left and right.

He nodded, understanding my worry about sentries.

We moved slower, stopping only behind the scaly trunks of large pines. Abruptly, Sheriff Bonner grabbed my arm and nodded off to his left.

I squinted into the patchy darkness. At the shadowy base of a pine several yards distant was another shadow, this one interrupting the vertical line of the trunk. Sheriff Bonner tapped his chest, then made a sweeping gesture to his left, indicating his route behind the Comanche sentry.

As he disappeared into the darkness, I crouched behind a pine and studied the silhouettes of other pines along the ridge, searching for another tell-tale shadow breaking the profile of the trunk. I saw nothing.

I looked back at the sentry, waiting. I flexed my

fingers around the rifle grip, taking some comfort in the way it fit into my hand.

Without warning, a shadow arose behind the sentry, then dropped over him. There came a soft moan, and one of the shadows disappeared.

Moments later, Bonner crawled out from the darkness. "He won't give the word."

I nodded. "Let's take a look first. My pa always warned me not to kick a fresh cow patty on a hot day."

Bonner grunted.

Together we eased forward until we spotted the camp. We dropped to our bellies and studied the layout.

The fire had burned low. I counted fourteen bodies wrapped in blankets and sprawled on the ground near the fire. A few Indian ponies stood hipshot among the sleeping warriors, tethered to their owner's ankles by lengths of woven rawhide. Beyond, in a natural valley formed by the juncture of the ridges, stood the stolen horses, most of them sleeping. Two young boys, not yet men, watched them.

Bonner leaned toward me. "Well, what about our cow patty?"

Without taking my eyes from the camp, I whispered, "I think we're about to kick it."

"Me too. Now you've seen what your troubles are, Mister Walker. You mind going back and bringing the others up?"

I looked at him. I couldn't make out his eyes, but I figured they were laughing. With a soft chuckle, I replied. "Won't mind a bit, Sheriff." My voice grew serious. "Just you watch yourself, you hear?"

"Yeah, I hear."

I sent Speck to bring Cranky and the horses up, then led the other five back to Bonner. He counted heads as we knelt by him. "Who's missing?"

"Speck. I sent him to bring up Cranky with the ponies. They're at least a mile back. I don't cotton to being on foot when we hit."

The sheriff nodded. "Me neither. Okay, boys. Spread out and keep watch."

The next fifteen minutes dragged. Below, the camp slumbered. I caught my breath when a warrior rose and tossed some logs on the fire. I released it slowly when he crawled back into his blankets.

Each movement, each sound, startled us. Even if we surprised them, we would instantly be at a severe disadvantage as long as we were without our ponies. I wasn't the only one worried. Arch kept glancing over his shoulder.

Rising into a crouch, Bonner waved us back. "Ponies ought to be close. Let's us find them, and then go amongst the heathens."

We ghosted back along the ridge, figments of imagination, shadowy wraiths flitting from tree to tree, more Indian than the Indian himself. The same mixed feeling of fear and excitement that I had experienced time and again during the War of Oppression coursed through my veins. I flexed my fingers around the grip of the Yellowboy Henry rifle.

Ahead loomed the shadows of our ponies.

Bonner growled. "Pinch them nostrils, boys. Don't want none of these hammer-headed cayuses to give us away. We'll lead them in until we're right on top of the camp."

One thing I had to say for Sheriff Bonner, he was bound and determined to slice the meat close to the bone.

I wished for my dun. I knew him. I knew exactly what he would do when the excitement and confusion of a gunfight broke out. The sorrel I was leading had been sound and dependable so far, but I had no idea what he would do when all Hades broke loose.

"Reckon I'll just find out," I muttered.

Next to me, Arch whispered, "What'd you say?"

"Nothing." I shook my head. "Just saying a little prayer."

He chuckled nervously. "That's all I been doing."

Bonner pulled up. From the shadows surrounding him came his voice. "Let's mount up, boys. Arch, you and Speck ride straight through the camp and try to circle the horses. The rest of us will give them Comanche more trouble than they ever figured possible."

Arch glanced at me.

"Take care," I whispered.

"You too."

I swung into the saddle. I held the reins in my left hand, the Henry in my right. Setting my heels in the stirrup, I stood up in the saddle once or twice, hoping the movement wouldn't startle my pony. He remained motionless.

Without a word, the eight of us lined up side by side, staring down at the Comanche camp fifty yards distant. Sheriff Bonner cried out, "Okay, boys. Let's open the show."

Eight saddle rifles roared, belching yellow plumes. As one we broke out with high-pitched howls and blazing rifles as we changed down the ridge onto the camp.

The sleeping camp erupted into a turmoil of confusion and chaos. Startled Comanches leaped from their blankets, waving their own rifles above their heads. Frightened ponies dashed from the camp, dragging those unlucky Indians who had tethered the ponies to their ankles.

We hit the camp before a single Comanche knew the direction from which we were charging.

The noise was deafening. Above the cacophony of roaring rifles came the shouts and curses of stunned warriors and raging cowboys. Horses squealed. Men shouted.

We charged through the camp, wheeled about, and charged again. I stood in my stirrups with the Henry jammed into my shoulder. Aiming was impossible, for the galloping pony beneath me bounced the muzzle of my rifle up and down and sideways.

All any of us could do was fire randomly, knowing that chances were remote that we would hit anything other than the ground or an unlucky pine. At least, we would make a lot of noise and scatter the Indians.

We spun around for a third charge. By now the camp was in shambles. Nevertheless, we spurred our ponies, gave out a nerve-grating Confederate cry, and barreled down again on the camp, firing as we went.

Without warning, a heavy object struck my shoulder, knocking me from the saddle and sending me rolling through the fire, which erupted into a explosion of sparks. I rolled to my feet and looked around to see a savage Comanche stick a revolver in my face and pull the trigger.

I froze as the old revolver misfired.

Before he could thumb back the hammer for a second attempt, I slapped his hand aside and slammed a fist into the middle of his forehead, sending him stumbling backward into the fire.

He shouted and jumped aside. I grabbed for my own sixgun, but by the time I had it out, he had vanished into the thick vegetation at the base of the ridge.

I hastily looked around for my pony. He was standing ground-reined beyond the fire. Cocking my sixgun, I ran to him, glancing first one way and then the other. By now, the battle had spread as the desperate Comanche climbed the ridges and raced down the gullies in an effort to disappear into the night.

Gathering the reins, I swung into the saddle.

Suddenly, Arch shouted at me. "Jed! Look out!"

I wheeled about just in time to see a grim-faced

Comanche racing toward me on horseback wielding a lance, its point five feet from my chest.

In the same instant, the boom of a rifle sounded, and the Comanche was knocked from his saddle, jerking the lance with him.

All I could do was stare at the dead Indian, stunned with the suddenness of the last few moments. Arch rode up, Winchester in hand. "That was close, Jed. You all right?"

I just shook my head, too numb to reply. Finally, I found my voice. "Yeah. Yeah, Arch. I'm just fine." When I did tear my eyes from the Comanche, I looked at Arch. The few chunks of wood still blazing lit his face. "Thanks."

He gave me a somber grin. "You'd do the same."

Gathering the horses, we headed back to the Bar H.

I had no idea what my next step might be, but I wasn't too worried. Like the past, I'd just keep plodding along. Something would turn up.

But for the first time in twelve years, I was reluctant to leave a place behind. It was the same feeling I had for my own home, years ago. I liked it, and I didn't want to leave.

Chapter Five

Stillman healed fast, and the next couple weeks passed quickly. I was developing a fondness for the Bar H. The old man was brusque, but fair. Mary Catherine—well, I was smitten with her. Of course, Red showed up every other day or so, still convinced he owned her. And the truth was, other than a smile or two from her, she gave me no indication that she wasn't Red's property.

Arch and I worked well together, like matching horses in harness. I never spoke much of my past, and he never inquired. Asking too many question of a stranger was considered poor manners, just like prying into a friend's business.

While snow seldom fell in East Texas during February or March, the weather remained chilly and wet, broken every couple weeks by two or three unseasonably warm days.

One night when a cold drizzle was falling, I sat at a poker table in the bunkhouse with Arch, Speck, and Cranky. The pot-bellied stove put out a satisfying glow of heat, seeming somehow even more comforting with the icy drizzle beating against the windows.

I was an old hand at poker, having played with Pa and my brother since I was ten. I knew just about every sleight of hand, every method of stacking the deck, and just about every trick to hide cards on my person. I knew how to use the pipe reflector and the ring shiners as well as the matchbox shiners. Pa taught us, not so we would cheat, but so no card slick could take advantage of us. Pa had a favorite saying: "Look out for the one-eyed man in the game," which meant watch out for cheats.

Often, William and I played just to pass the long nights. Those were our cheating games, when we each tried to out-slick the other. Our eyes became as sharp as our fingers were deft.

And it was a skill I had put to good practice during the War of Oppression.

Now I played the game for fun. My three opponents were not accomplished card players. I had no trouble picking up the peculiar quirks and tell-tale signs that told me what they had in mind. I had no intention of cleaning their pockets. On the other hand, I had no intention of letting them clean mine.

As with most card games among acquaintances, idle questions were batted back and forth.

Cranky was the oldest of the group, going on his mid-forties.

"What do you mean, you ain't sure how old you be?" Speck snapped, grinning.

"Just what I says. I never had me no family. Ain't no way I can know for sure. All I know is I was a younker when Houston took care of that Mexican, Santa Ana." He paused and studied his hand. "Reckon I'll take two cards." While Arch dealt the cards, Cranky looked over the coal oil lamp at me. "Whereabouts you from, Jed? You don't talk like folks around here."

"Missouri." I looked at Speck. "I'll take one card."

Arch looked up sharply, then quickly shifted his gaze back to his cards.

Cranky whistled. "I onct worked with an old boy from Missouri." He shook his head. "Stubbornest mule I ever met."

We all laughed, and Speck bet a quarter. Arch raised another quarter. Cranky bumped the pot another quarter, and I called.

Cranky took the pot.

Later that night, Arch whispered from the darkness of the room, "Jed, it ain't none of my business, but those men you are looking for—what'd they do?" He hesitated and added, "Have anything to do with your brother?"

In the past, whenever someone started nosing into my past, the hackles on the back of my neck bristled. This time was different. For some reason, his question did not offend me. I stared into the darkness above my head.

He continued. "You don't have to tell me if you don't cotton to it. I was just wondering, thinking I might be of some help."

I turned my head on the pillow and stared in his direction. "Strange. For some reason, it don't bother me. I'm not really sure why. But, I reckon you got a right to know. After all, you kept me from wearing a war lance through my chest."

Arch chuckled. "Just happened to be at the right place at the right time."

"Well, I'm mighty glad of that."

"Me too, Jed. Me too."

He grew silent, and I knew he was waiting. "Ain't a whole heap to tell. Born and raised in Missouri, down near Indian Territory. Ma died when I was about ten or so. Pa about four years later. That left William and me. He was two years older, but we managed. We put together a small herd and headed for the Shawnee Trail, figuring to sell them to one of the drives heading to the railhead. Bushwhackers jumped us. Left us for dead. I made it. William didn't. I swore then I'd find them that ambushed us, all five of them."

For several seconds, Arch remained silent. Finally, in a thin, almost unrecognizable voice, he mumbled, "I thought you said there was only three."

My blood ran cold as I relived those first few years. "I was only sixteen, but I was smart enough to know I didn't have skills to take care of them then, so I spent the next three years getting ready." I paused, remembering those days. In the darkness, I could hear Arch's shallow breathing. I continued. "The first one I found outside of St. Louis. The second during the war at Chattanooga. He was a Reb too, but that didn't matter. Blood kin comes first. Now, the third one is dead."

His voice trembled. "You mean the one the Comanches killed back north of Nacogdoches?"

I just figured it was the chill that made his voice shake like it did. "That's what I reckon. He heard me ask about the one with the scar. I can't figure no other reason for the ambush. With him gone, that leaves two. The one with a scar and the other one."

Arch's voice was hesitant. "What did he look like?"

I sighed. "I don't know. He was young. That's all I remember. Before I kill Scarface, I'll make him tell me."

We grew silent. I listened to the patter of icy drizzle on the pine shake roof. The fire on the hearth burned low. Finally, I slept. I dreamed of Scarface.

Next morning was bitterly cold, with a driving rain. The dark clouds tumbled just above the tips of the towering pines. Buttoning my slicker tight and turning up my collar, I pulled my hat down over my ears and slogged through the mud to the barn to tend my horse.

While I was graining him, the doors swung open

and Arch hurried inside, followed by a stranger leading a bedraggled horse. "Find a spot for your pony over there, stranger. Then come on back to the house for some grub." Arch spotted me. "Morning, Jed," he mumbled, quickly turning to tend his own horse. Over his shoulder, he added, "Jed, this here is John Smith. You all come on up for breakfast when you finish," he said, hurrying from the barn. I puzzled a moment at his brusque behavior, but I just figured he had something important on his mind.

The stranger looked like a drowned cat. His hat brim was beat down about his ears. "Howdy," I said, giving him a nod.

He dipped his head at me and pulled off his soaked hat. It was a round crown, the style from up north. His long hair fell down on his shoulders. "Howdy."

We made idle talk until he finished drying and graining his pony, and then together we dashed through the rain for the kitchen.

Stillman and some of the hands had already wolfed down their vittles, but as usual, there was a heap left. Nothing gives a cold body more pleasure on a cold, wet morning that fried venison, fried potatoes, hot biscuits, steaming red-eye gravy, and boiling hot six-shooter coffee. It sticks to your ribs and warms your insides all good and satisfying.

I glanced across the table at John Smith, who was nothing but elbows as he dug into his grub. *John Smith*, I said to myself with a heavy dose of cynicism. During my years on the trail, I'd run into dozens of

John Smiths, all sharing a common hope of escaping the law.

Arch usually sat across the table from me, but this morning, he sat at the other end. He addressed the newcomer. "Been on the trail long?"

Smith paused with a forkful of biscuit dripping with gravy in mid-air. "Couple days. Come from up Shelby County. Old partner of mine from Montana sent word he had a job for me down at Sumter in Trinity County down southwest of here." He poked the biscuit in his mouth and muttered while he chewed. "Ain't many jobs to be had around these parts, from what I hear."

Arch shook his head. "Not many. We been having all we can do to keep the Yankee carpetbaggers from our door."

Wiping the gravy from his lips with the back of his hand, Smith nodded. "That's what I heard from a gal in a saloon—" He hesitated and shot an apologetic glance at Mary Catherine, who was standing by the stove. "Beg pardon, ma'am. I didn't mean to speak like that in front of a woman."

With a brief nod and faint smile, she turned back to the stove.

Smith looked back to us and continued. "I was at a table having myself a game of stud with a little jasper with a missing finger. He was talking about—"

I caught my breath, unable to believe my ears. I looked up sharply. "What was that? Who did you say?"

Smith frowned at me, clearly puzzled. "About what?"

"You said something about a jasper with a missing finger."

He nodded and took another bite of grub. "Yeah. Small hombre. Wore a black slicker." Gravy dripped from the fork when he pointed it at his little finger. "He was missing this finger on his left hand."

"When?"

"Huh?" Smith looked at Arch, then back at me, confused by the sudden urgency in my tone.

"I said, when did you see this cowpoke?" I slid away from the table and stood up, glaring down at him. "When did you see him?" I asked again, my voice cold and demanding.

"Why—I reckon it was only two, maybe three days ago up in Shelbyville. We was sitting at—"

I turned to Arch. "I'd be obliged if I could buy a supply of vittles."

He stared at me a moment, his eyes wide. Suddenly he shook his head. "You think it's the same one?"

"How many cowboys you know with a little finger missing?"

"Then who was it the Comanche killed on the north trace?"

I shook my head. "Got no idea, but I got no choice here."

He glanced at Mary Catherine, then nodded to me. "You get your soogan ready. I'll pack some grub for your saddlebags."

I looked back at Smith. "Which way did he ride out?"

Frowning, Smith shrugged. "I reckon I left town before he did. If he did ride out, it wasn't down the trace to Nacogdoches."

Mary Catherine was already rolling out an oilcloth as I left the kitchen.

After poking my gear in my soogan, I rolled it up tight against the weather. Arch came in and packed the grub in my saddlebags. I noticed he had trouble looking me in the eye. "You want me to go with you?" There was a strange look in his eyes, almost sad.

I paused and grinned at him. "Much obliged. This is something I got to do myself."

"You got plenty of cartridges?"

"Yep." I slung my soogan over my shoulder and reached for the saddlebags.

He pulled them back. "No. I'll carry them out to the barn for you. That's the least I can do."

Five minutes later, I swung into the saddle and looked down at Arch. For the first time in the twelve years since William was shot down, I felt the stirrings of regret over leaving the Bar H.

He forced his eyes to mine. "I'd really like to ride along with you, Jed. I can be ready in five minutes."

I leaned over and stuck out my hand. "Thanks. Like I said, this is my hand to play." I wanted to say more, to ask more, but it wasn't my place.

He squeezed my hand. "I need to—what I mean is, when you finish your job, you're welcome here."

I don't reckon I could have spoken a word anyway for the lump in my throat, so I just nodded and rode out. As I rode past the house, I spotted Mary Catherine standing at the window. She raised her hand as I rode by. I touched my finger to the brim of my hat and nudged my spurs into my dun pony.

Chapter Six

The narrow trace northeast of Nacogdoches wound for forty miles through the thick forest of pine and oak, climbing over rolling hills and circling around sheer bluffs of red hardpan. The icy rain continued, churning the red soil into a thick sludge.

I rode with my head ducked into the rain. Not once did I chide myself for not remaining at the Bar H until the weather let. I had no choice. The jasper with the missing finger might already have ridden out of Shelbyville.

An hour before dark, I came upon an old live oak felled by some ancient storm. The forks in the tree had jammed into the ground, supporting the thick trunk. The soil had been washed from the root ball, and the bare roots jabbed into the air like witch's fingers. Over the years, the surrounding oaks and pines had dropped their leaves and needles, almost covering the oak. Beneath the forks, I spotted as snug a camp as I figured I would find on a day like this.

By dark, I'd rigged a canvas roof and dragged in a heap of dry needles on which to toss my soogan. To my surprise, Arch had packed a small coffeepot and small bag of ground Arbuckle's coffee.

Despite the weather, I was fairly comfortable. The rain that dripped through the canvas and needles hit the tarp on my soogan, so I was nice and dry. That, with a fully belly of venison and biscuits washed down with hot coffee, was all a jasper like me could ask for.

After I finished my small meal, I pulled my quilts around my neck and stared at the small fire.

There's no time more suited for a hombre to reflect on his own being than when he's all by his lonesome at night in the middle of the wilderness. I had lost count of the times I sat around a campfire trying to take all that was going on about me and fit it into what was supposed to be.

An eye for an eye.

I was beginning to wonder. I'd spent twelve years in pursuit of that charge. Was this supposed to be a lifelong quest like some of those old Greeks and Romans I'd read about in Pa's books?

Ma was the religious one in our house. She believed in the Old Testament, and she was bound and determined that William and I would also be religious. The only time she'd take a switch to us was if we didn't read twenty verses from the Bible every night.

Now, Pa was the one who could have really used all that Bible reading, but Bill and me never dared whisper the thought.

Bill was twelve and I was ten when Ma died of the cholera. Pa buried her good and proper, then went on a two-week drunk. Me and Bill kept the farm going. Four years later, Pa died when a wagonload of corn seed fell on him and the axle crushed his chest.

William and me buried Pa and went back to work.

Two years later, bushwhackers shot us up and stole our small herd that wouldn't have brought more than a hundred dollars from even the most generous of buyers.

I never figured that to be much of a bargain—a brother for a hundred dollars.

During the night, the rain ceased and the wind let up. The sun rose next morning in a sky as blue as a robin's egg. I put the leftover coffee on to boil while I fed and saddled my dun. Within ten minutes, I was back on the trace, heading northeast to Shelbyville.

I rode into the small village just before dark. It was nothing more than a few rough log cabins on either side of the road. In the middle of the cabins on the north side of the road sat a lone structure of rough-hewn pine planks, the general store and saloon. At the end of the row was the livery, an unchinked log structure that let in more rain than it kept out.

A dim yellow glow from the barn lantern inside the

livery struggled against the encroaching darkness. I dismounted and led my dun inside. An old man, his legs so bowed you could shove a barrel between them, rose unsteadily from his seat on a keg in front of a pot-bellied stove and grunted. "Howdy."

I nodded, taking in the almost empty livery at a glance. "Got room for my pony?"

He pointed a gnarled and twisted finger into the darkness beyond the flickering lantern. "Two bits. Another two bits for grain." He slipped a pint bottle of whiskey from his hip pocket and drained what little remained.

I flipped him the coins, then stabled my dun. After rubbing him down, I had to dig through the grain to find some that wasn't moldy. Last thing I needed was an ailing horse.

The old man watched idly as I rubbed my horse down, dried my rig best I could, and slung my soogan over a rail. I gestured to the loft. "Any charge for throwing my bed up there for the night?"

He hooked his thumb over his shoulder. "You going over to the saloon?"

I glanced out the door at the dim lights across the street. "Reckon so."

"Bring me a drink. You can throw your soogan down here by the fire."

With a grin, I shrugged. "Sounds fair." I paused. "I'm looking for a man. Short." I held my hand out at shoulder height. "About this tall, skinny, wearing a black slicker, and the little finger on his left hand is missing."

The old livery man studied me a moment with his filmy blue eyes. "How long back?"

"Five or six days now, I reckon."

"They was this one feller. Never talked to him, but he wore a black slicker. He was around a few days. I ain't seen him lately." He nodded to the general store and saloon. "Pooch Brewster owns the saloon. Maybe he can tell you something."

I saw where Pooch got his nickname. Put him side by side with a floppy-jowled basset hound and a jasper would be hard put to tell the difference. He slid me a drink of whiskey. I tossed it down and nodded for another. While he poured, I asked him about the small gent.

He paused, eyeing me warily. "You the law?"

"No. Just trying to do a favor for a friend."

He nodded as he corked the bottle. "Yep. I remember the feller. Called hisself Abner. Don't reckon that was his real name. Come in afoot. Seems someone along the trace hijacked him and robbed him blind, even took his horse. He swamped out the place for me for a couple days."

I looked around the room. The general store began at the end of the bar. "He still around?"

Pooch shook his head. His jowls flopped back and forth. "Nope. Got in a card game and won enough to buy a horse. Rode out day before yesterday."

Sipping my whiskey, I asked, "You know which way he headed?"

He paused, eyeing me suspiciously. "What did you say you were looking for him for?"

Lying was not my strong suit, but I gave it a shot. I said the first thing that came to my mind. "Friend down in Nacogdoches wanted me to let him know that they caught the jasper that stole his horse. The sheriff is keeping the horse in the livery. A strawberry roan."

Pooch nodded, convinced of my truthfulness.

I was surprised myself. Lying wasn't so hard after all.

"He said he wanted to get to Galveston. I figure he probably headed east to Round Bend Landing on the Sabine River. Water's high enough there should be some boats heading downriver."

I downed my whiskey, bought a tin of crackers and a can of peaches, and then remembered my promise to the old livery man. "Give me a couple shots in an old bottle."

Pooch frowned, then a grin of understanding spread over his face. "Old Lew talked you into some whiskey, huh?"

"Lew?"

He pointed out the door. "At the livery."

"Yeah. Got my pony there. Two drinks gets me the ground by the fire." I pulled my coat tight around my neck. "Going to be mighty cold tonight."

"Reckon so," Pooch replied, pouring a generous two

slugs in a bottle. "I put a little extra in there, partner. Like you said, it's going to be mighty cold tonight."

I buttoned up and cradled the bag of supplies in my arm. As I reached for the front door, it slammed open, knocking me backward and spilling the groceries over the floor. "What the—"

Two young cowpokes strode in. Ignoring me, the one in front called out, "Hey, Pooch, pull out a bottle. We're ready for some fun."

Pooch shouted back, "Watch where you're going, Billy Ray. You almost knocked that gent down."

Billy Ray laughed. "He ain't hurt, Pooch." He turned and sneered at me, his cheeks red and his eyes glassy from too much whiskey. "Hey, cowboy. You best watch where you're going if you don't want to get hurt. Them doors can be mighty dangerous weapons."

"Yeah," his friend chimed in, laughing. "You ought to stop stumbling over your own clodhoppers."

Well, I always knew it didn't take a genius to spot a goat in a flock of sheep, and I could tell right now that there was likely to be a heap of excitement around here in the next few minutes.

I glanced at my groceries strewn on the floor. My ears burned. I clenched my fists once or twice and forced myself to relax. They were youngsters, full of vinegar. Smartest move was to let it pass. I'd be out of here in the morning, and I'd forget all about them.

"Well, boys, I reckon you're right. Old boy like me

gets clumsy every once in a while." I dropped to one knee and reached for the can of peaches.

Billy Ray drawled. "Well, now Dub, don't that cowboy look right at home down there?"

Pooch spoke up. "That's enough, Billy Ray. Back off."

But the young man ignored the bartender. He sauntered over to where I was picking up the groceries and stopped. "Just you hush up, Pooch. Else I'll say a word to my pa." He slid his muddy boot forward. "While you're down there, cowboy, clean the mud off my boots."

I paused, the can of peaches in my hand. "Why, sure, son. Here, catch this for me." I tossed the can of peaches straight up over his head.

"Huh? What?" He took a step back and grabbed for the can.

I shot up from where I was kneeling, bringing my right fist whistling up from the floor. Poor dumb Billy Ray's jaw was wide open when I smashed my knotted fist into it. He dropped like a sack of feed.

"Hey," shouted Dub, taking a step toward us.

Without hesitation, I twisted at the waist and slung a sizzling left hook that would have torn Dub's head clean off if his body had not twisted after him. He slammed into the floor face down. A pool of blood spread from around his head.

Pooch shuffled up. In a lazy, disinterested tone, he drawled. "Lord, Mister. I do think old Dub there busted his nose when he hit the floor."

I stooped over and picked up the rest of my goods. "Yep," I replied, tugging the can of peaches from Billy Ray's rigid fingers. "Them wood floors will mess up a nose every time like that."

He chuckled. "They both be spoiled brats. Does a body good to see them get what they deserve." He looked up at me and grew serious. "Billy Ray's pa is the big toad in the pond around here. He could cause you some trouble."

I tugged my coat around my neck against the cold. "Well, if he plans on it, he'd best put a hitch in his get-along. I'm riding out before sunup."

Pooch nodded, studying the two motionless figures on the floor. Without a word, he pulled two folded blankets off a shelf and spread them over the boys. "I'll just let'em sleep here tonight."

Chapter Seven

If Pooch had been a fortune-teller, he would have died a rich man. His prediction came true next morning as I was saddling up.

A rock-jawed hombre with a badge pinned to his Mackinaw strode through the livery door. Behind him was a red-faced cowboy about middle age and two sheepish boys. The sheriff stopped in the middle of the livery. "You. Cowboy!"

I peered over the saddle as I finished tightening the cinch. "What can I do for you, Sheriff?"

"You the jasper what whipped up on these boys?"

"If you mean did I give them a well-deserved lesson in manners, yeah."

Without taking his eyes off me, he spoke over his shoulder. "This the one?"

"That's him, Sheriff," babbled Billy Ray, who

turned to his pa. "Like I told you, Pa. He caught us when we wasn't looking. Why—"

"Shut up, boy. All right, Sheriff. Do your duty. Arrest him."

Like magic, a shiny hogleg appeared in the sheriff's hand. "That's what I aim to do, Mister Rangel. Just you leave it to me. All right, cowboy. Just you unsaddle that pony and come with me. And don't cause me no trouble. We don't like saddle tramps causing us no trouble."

I'd never pulled down on the law, and I didn't plan on it now, no matter how much it pained me to be delayed like this, especially because of two wet-behind-the-ears crybabies. I took a deep breath and nodded. "No trouble, Sheriff. Whatever you say." I figured I'd only lose a couple hours. Abner, if that was his name, couldn't get too far ahead in two hours.

The two hours turned into two weeks.

That's how long it took the judge to reach us on his circuit.

Despite his stubborn and persnickety interpretation of the law, the sheriff was a fair man. He turned me loose during the day to take care of my horse and clean out the livery and do other odd jobs to pay for my pony's keep.

During one of those days, a lanky man in a black frock coat and pants wearing a boiled shirt under a checked vest stopped in the livery and introduced himself as Stephen Wilson Houston, a distant relative of old Sam Houston. He was a lawyer, and according to him, if I was going to face the Catalog Judge, I sure needed representation.

"The Catalog Judge? What the sam hill you talking about, Mister Houston?"

Houston pulled out a twist of tobacco and worried off a chunk. He handed it to me, but I passed it up. I had enough bad habits without dribbling tobacco juice down the front of my shirt. "Well, son. Old Erwin Adams is a right fair judge for certain folk. He ain't one of them carpetbagger judges. He's one of us. Now, he sees clean though most artifices. He——"

"Through what?"

Houston cleared his throat. "Artifices. You know, tricks, ploys, lies."

"Oh."

"Anyway, like I was saying, most of the time, he sees through the tricks folks play if they ain't important people like old man Rangel. If they are important—well, personally, I figure you're going to be found guilty. I'd like to keep that from happening."

The old livery man came in through the back door, reached behind a post next to the wall, and pulled out a bottle of Old Orchard whiskey. He took a long pull, then handed it to me. I followed suit, and showing proper manners, handed it to Houston. Not being one to hurt anyone's feelings, he took a healthy gulp and handed it back to Lew.

I cleared my throat. "Why you doing this for me, Mister Houston?"

Lew snorted. " 'Cause him and Rangel hate each other. Have for twenty years."

The accusation did not faze Houston. He pursed his lips. "The gentleman is correct, Mister Walker. I do not deny it." He reached for the bottle, and Lew supplied it. After a long swig, he held his fingers to his lips and gave a discreet burp. "I will do anything I possibly can to put a burr under Bob Rangel's saddle. If I can keep the judge from finding you guilty, I'll be in hog heaven. Even if you're found guilty, I'll enjoy nettling old Bob."

Well, I supposed that some lawyers had worse reasons for representing a body, but at least Stephen Wilson Houston was honest. "Tell me, Mister Houston. Why do you call him the Catalog Judge?"

Arching his eyebrows, he replied, "Why, that's because if he fines you, he takes the amount of the fine from the Monkey Ward catalog."

I considered the matter. "I appreciate the offer, but the truth is, Mister Houston, I don't know how I can pay you. I'm so broke, why I can't even pay attention."

He chuckled. "How much you got on you, boy?"

"Five dollars and some change."

"That's exactly what I charge."

I grinned. Stephen Wilson Houston was my kind of man.

By the time Judge Adams arrived, I'd made several friends in Shelbyville. In a way, I was going to hate to leave.

Court was held in the saloon, which had been closed down for the trial. Houston had Judge Adams pegged when it came to kowtowing to the more influential townfolk. No sooner had he taken his seat than he pounded on the table and said, "Now, Mister Walker, you got anything to say before I find you guilty?"

Well, sir, that was Steve Houston's signal. He jumped up and objected. Then Rangel jumped up and objected to Houston's objection.

The whole town was in the gallery, and I heard later that some of the more unscrupulous were placing bets on everything from how many times Houston would throw out an objection to when Bob Rangel would blow up.

Finally, Pooch took the stand to testify. He told it like it happened. Judge Adams eyed him narrowly. "Now, Pooch, you sure you just ain't saying that because you never liked Billy Ray Rangel?"

"No sir, Judge. I'm under oath. I ain't lying even if Billy Ray is a rotten brat."

Bob Rangel jumped up and objected again.

That's how the trial went for another hour. I testified. The sheriff testified as to how I had caused no trouble and was a good and faithful inmate. Lew the livery man stayed sober long enough to say some good things about me and how the two young cowpokes deserved more of what I gave them.

Judge Adams listened to it all, then after a lengthy deliberation that lasted all of two seconds, pronounced, "Guilty as charged."

Houston raised an appeal.

Rangel objected.

Adams ignored them both. He pounded his gavel on the table. "Will the prisoner rise?" He reached into his saddlebags and pulled out the catalog. "Mister Smith, I ain't sentencing you to no jail time because them boys probably deserved what they got, but I ain't having nobody going around my jurisdiction and causing trouble. Therefore, I'm fining you—" He paused and flipped through the pages. He jabbed his finger at a page and grinned. "I'm fining you three dollars and ninety-five cents."

Rangel exploded. "That ain't fair, Judge! Look what he done to my boy."

I glanced down at Steve Houston. "Three dol—"

He hushed me with a whisper. "Just be glad he stopped at pants and not at pianos."

For several seconds, I considered his observation. I nodded and sat back down. That made as much sense as anything else had around here. I leaned over. "After I pay the fine, Mister Houston, I'll only have a dollar and some change."

He looked across the room at Bob Rangel, whose face looked like a boiler ready to explode. When Houston turned back to me, an expression of supreme contentment was on his face. "A dollar and some change? Why, that's exactly my charge."

After paying Houston his fee, I was broke. I wrangled a few dollars from Lew the liveryman by doing some saddle swapping. Then I lost no time hightailing it out of Shelbyville, taking the east trace for Round Bend Landing on the Sabine. The weather was favorable, and after two weeks of inactivity, me and the dun were ready to stretch our legs.

Round Bend Landing was a pier that stretched along the riverbank about a hundred feet or so. On the low bluff behind the pier was a single building of weathered clapboard with a pine shake roof.

The owner was as friendly as a puppy dog. Over a glass or three of cheap whiskey, I managed to find out that Abner had passed through two weeks earlier. Upon discovering no water transportation, he headed downriver to Hackmann's Ferry, where shallow draft steamboats put in regularly about once a month.

I bought some flour and salt. Those items, with the last of the coffee Arch had given me, would have to hold me until I reached Hackmann's.

The narrow trail twisted and turned. When it turned west, I continued south straight through the forest, figuring that sooner or later I'd either run across the road or reach Hackmann's.

There was little growth on the floor of the pine and oak forest, since the canopy of leaves overhead prevented the sunlight from reaching the ground. But, in those areas ravaged by storms that snapped great pines in half and toppled giant oaks, the vegetation grew thicker than seven cowpokes on a cot. I'd never had problems keeping my directions straight, but those thickets were so tangled that at times the only way I knew I was heading south was by keeping the sound of the river on my left.

Along the riverbank bluffs were deep gullies cut by centuries of runoff water draining from the forest into the river. Near dark, I found a hollow cut back into the side of a deep gulch that offered an ideal camp. A tangle of undergrowth so thick a rabbit couldn't wind his way through it surrounded the gully. Overhead, the wind hummed through the treetops, but down on the forest floor, all was still.

I rolled out my soogan in the back of the hollow where the heat from the small fire collected. My supper of hot coffee and fried flour might not have made the menu at the Palmer House in Chicago, but I doubt if there was any room in that hotel that was any warmer or more snug than my soogan that night against the bitter cold.

Before I drifted off to sleep, I thought back about Arch, and just how peculiar he had behaved that last day. I couldn't figure out if I did something wrong or what had happened. When we went to bed, he was fine. All we talked about was the bushwhackers. But I didn't see how that could have bothered him.

I pulled out early next morning, bundled in my Mackinaw and my button-up slicker. Deciding to avoid the thickets near the river where the sunlight reached, I rode into the forest, taking advantage of the easy travel under the tall pine and oaks. The sun was not yet up, but the gray light of false dawn filled the forest.

I ran across the road from Round Bend Landing to Hackmann's. It was still as serpentine as a ten-foot corn snake, so instead of following it, I continued due south, opting for more of the smooth path under the great oaks and giant pines.

From time to time, I'd hear the rustle of leaves and needles as deer moved through the dark woods From overhead, in the limbs and branches of the spreading oaks and sentinel pines, came the cheery warbling of the wood thrushes and sparrows, interrupted by the raucous jabbering of the bluejays.

We, the animals and me, weren't much different from each other. They were forced from their warm beds and nests to forage for food just as I was forced to stay on the trail of the little man with the missing finger.

Mid-morning, a distant gunshot off to the southwest startled me. I jerked my dun to a halt and shucked my own sixgun. I froze, staring through the forest in the direction of the shot. Two more shots followed, deeper sounding, like the old trade rifles unscrupulous traders swapped the Indians for blankets.

A single shot followed, then silence.

Slowly, I made my way forward.

Pa had taught me never to interfere with something that wasn't bothering me. That made good sense. My only problem here was the possibility that whatever was taking place out there might turn around to put some bother on me later.

So I rode southwest, wishing now for some of those thickets I left back near the river. My pony's ears perked forward. I jerked him a halt. I squinted into the distance, trying to see what caught his attention. Moments later, a few shadows crossed from my right to left, heading for the river.

I slipped from the saddle, holstering my Colt. "Easy, boy," I whispered, rubbing the dun's neck with one hand while gently pinching his nostrils with the other to keep him from whinnying.

The shadows moved slowly. I knew they must be scanning the forest and I hoped I was lost in the shadows around me. I remained motionless for several minutes after they disappeared. Finally, I released my hold on my horse and realized beads of sweat were running down my face.

I whistled softly and reached for my canteen. I poured some water into the cup of my hand and held it under my pony's nose. He slurped it up, and then I took a large drink and popped the cork back in it. "Okay, fella. Let's see what was going on over there."

When we hit the trail, my blood ran cold. Unshod ponies. Indians. My Texas experience had been with the Comanche, so I figured that's who they were. Maybe remnants of that war party we broke up back in January. I turned along their backtrail, which led directly towards a sheer bluff covered thick with vines and small shrubs. I studied the ground.

A patch of earth forty or fifty feet across was churned from the hooves of several ponies. From studying the ground, I guessed at least a dozen or more. I rode around the perimeter of the torn earth. Two more trails led into the forest, one to the west, the other north.

Slowly, I laid my hand on the butt of my sixgun. Three patrols of Indians heading out in different directions. Did they plan on meeting back here? I studied the shadowy forest about me. They could be anywhere out there. I muttered a curse.

Suddenly a soft whistle broke the stillness of the air. I shucked my sixgun, figuring it was an Indian signal, that they'd spotted me.

A voice just above a whisper called out. "Up here. Look up here, Mister."

Not quite halfway up the fifty-foot bluff, a face peered out through the thick growth of vines.

I couldn't believe my eyes.

He stuck his arm out and gestured to the south side of the bluff. "Over there. Meet me over there."

And then he disappeared.

Chapter Eight

His name was Cyrus Miller, and he had found himself a snug little hidey-hole inside the bluff. There were two levels. The first was a cave large enough for half a dozen ponies with a shaft that led up to a second cave, about half the size. That's where we now stood.

"Pure accident I found it," he explained as we peered at the forest through a small opening hidden by the thick web of vines. "Just stumbled into it yesterday. This morning, I was out trying to scare up a rabbit or something when one of them Injuns spotted me. They lost my trail right outside where the ground is torn up."

I glanced around at him. Tow-headed, about fourteen, I guessed. Patched duds, worn brogans. "What are you doing out here, boy?" I asked.

He told me how he and his pa had been bush-

69

whacked, how he got himself good and lost, and how now he just wandered about, eating whatever didn't eat him.

I felt sorry for the boy. He'd had it rough, yet I'd often noticed that them who have it rugged often times manage to climb to the top of the heap ahead of those who have it all handed them.

"Well, Cyrus, I wish I had something decent to grub down on, but my belly's shaking hands with my backbone too. All I got is flour, and we can't afford a fire for the smoke."

"That makes me no mind. I ain't all that hungry."

I tossed him a blanket, and I took the other. We spent a cold, hungry night in the cave. I kept expecting the Indians to return, but they never did.

We rode out with the sun, heading for the river, Cyrus riding behind me. "We reach the river, we'll have a fire and some coffee. That way, if the Comanche decides to jump us, he can only come at us from one side."

But we saw no sign of any hostiles after we'd made the fire.

The hot coffee and fried flour didn't fill us up, but it was a tasty treat. I promised Cyrus that once we reached Hackmann's, I'd get us some meat.

Just before dark, we spotted Hackmann's Ferry. I only had a couple dollars, but I was ready to spend it for a decent meal for me and Cyrus.

Suddenly, I spotted a deer on the riverbank off to

my left. It was staring at us. Moving slowly as not to spook him, I slid my Yellowboy Henry from the boot.

Abruptly, the deer bolted. I swung the rifle butt into my shoulder and in the same movement lined the front sight on the bounding animal and squeezed the trigger.

"You got him," Cyrus shouted, sliding off the dun's rump and racing toward the fallen animal.

I swapped Hackmann the deer for some coffee, more flour, a slab of bacon, four cans of peaches, and half a dozen fried venison steaks for supper and breakfast.

I deliberately kept quiet about Abner. I figured on questioning Hackmann the next morning.

We spent a snug night on the floor in front of the fire with full bellies and grins on our faces. Next morning, while we gnawed on the fried venison, I asked Hackmann about Abner.

The ferryman had a greasy complexion that together with his fat lips and beer-keg belly made my skin crawl. "Sure. I remember the little guy. Sold me his horse to get boat fare on the *Captain Howard*."

"The *Captain Howard*." I glanced in the direction of the river. "I figured it was too shallow up here for a steamboat."

He shrugged. "Naw. Not this time of year. 'Course, the *Captain Howard* ain't one of them big kind. It's smaller."

I sipped my coffee and tried to appear casual. "You know where he was heading?"

"Naw." He dragged the back of his hand across his lips and wiped the grease on his thigh. "Friend of yours?"

"No." I fell back on the same lie I'd told up in Shelbyville. "Some jasper stole his horse over near Nacogdoches. Friend of his asked me to pass the word if I ran into him."

Hackmann picked at the food stuck between his teeth with his fingernail. "Oh."

"You might pass the word should he come back," I added, spreading a little frosting on the lie.

"Glad to."

I went out to saddle my pony. Cyrus tagged after me like a little puppy. I'd put off figuring out what to do with him, but now I had no choice. I had to decide something, so I put it to him.

"Well, Cyrus. What do we do with you now?"

His forehead wrinkled in disappointment. "I—well, I kinda figured on going with you."

I had a thousand reasons not to take him with me. And I told him every one of them. He just stood there, looking up at me, tears pooling in his eyes. "What about family? You got some somewhere, don't you?"

He shook his head and stared at the ground. "No. Ma died. It was just me and Pa. Them bushwhackers took all we had." A gust of wind flapped his loose-fitting pants about his skinny legs and stung his red cheeks.

I had to travel, and travel fast. I couldn't be tied down by a youngster. I glanced over his shoulder at

Hackmann's, wondering if he needed someone to work around the place. A picture of the fat, greasy proprietor flashed through my brain. No way I'd let the boy stay with him. Why, I reckon I would probably even have second thoughts about selling Hackmann a horse.

Then I remembered the Bar H. If only there was some way to get Cyrus to the Bar H. I scratched the stubble of beard on my jaw. Maybe I could take him downriver until I found a road to Nacogdoches. Maybe—

At that moment, two grizzled riders pulled up at the hitching rail in front of Hackmann's. Cyrus glanced around, then looked back at me, his eyes wide as pie pans. "Jed. That's them. They the ones that bushwhacked us. That sorrel is mine. And that's my saddle with my own leather reata I made myself. Pa burned my name under the saddle skirt."

I stared at him. "You sure, boy?"

He nodded emphatically. "The sorrel's name is Sarah. I raised her from a filly."

Now, I'm no fool. Only as a last resort will I go up against two hombres and try to outdraw them. I did what any smart jasper would do and slipped my Henry from the boot. Those .44 caliber slugs evened the odds. I clanked a cartridge into the chamber and stepped around the rear of my dun. "Get out of the way, Cyrus. Far back."

The two hombres were tying their ponies when Hackmann stepped on the porch. Before he could greet them, I spoke up. "Hold on, boys."

Forty or fifty feet separated us. They glared at me from under their turned-down brims. The slender one with a sepulcher face growled, "What's your problem, cowboy?" He eyed the Henry cradled in my arm.

"I got me a youngster here who claims you boys bushwhacked him and his pa. Killed his pa."

The second one, who was going to fat, laughed. "We ain't bushwhacked nobody."

"Maybe not," I replied. "But he claims that sorrel belongs to him. Saddle too."

The two cowpokes exchanged nervous looks. The thin one snarled, "He's crazy." But his fingers inched toward the butt of his sixgun.

"He says his name is on the saddle skirt."

"There ain't no name there," said the fat one. "He's making it all up."

"Well, boys. Maybe you're right. If you are, I'll apologize, but tell you what. Untie that sorrel. Throw the reins over her neck."

"What for?"

I cocked the Henry and pointed the muzzle at the fat one's belly. "To humor me."

Hackmann started to step forward. I barked at him. "This is none of your concern, barkeep. You step back. You're my witness."

I made a sharp gesture with the muzzle of the rifle at the fat cowpoke. "I said throw the reins over the saddle."

The two jaspers' eyes were darting every which way, like frightened animals. I knew then that Cyrus was right. They were the bushwhackers. Bushwhackers like the ones I had sought for years. I made a conscious effort to still my trembling muscles, to still the fury burning in my chest.

As the fat cowpoke slowly draped the reins over the saddle, the skinny one took a step aside. I stopped him in his tracks. "Hold it, partner. You stay where you are unless you want to start the show right now."

He said nothing. He glared at me and flexed his fingers.

The sorrel remained at the rail, head drooping. "Okay, boy. You say she's yours. Call her." I tightened my finger on the trigger.

Cyrus gave a piercing whistle. "Sarah. Here, girl."

The sorrel's head came up and her ears perked forward. With a nicker, she started trotting to Cyrus, taking a path directly between me and the skinny bushwhacker.

With a cry of anger, the fat one grabbed his sixgun.

I dropped to one knee and squeezed off a shot. The Henry roared and the two-hundred-grain slug slammed into the bushwhacker's chest, spinning him around to land face down on the ground.

Cursing, the second cowboy had to jump to one side so he could see around the sorrel. As soon as he came into sight behind her rump, I gave him the same dose of lead poisoning I had given his partner.

Hackmann stood motionless on the porch, his mouth open in shock.

The sorrel nuzzled up to Cyrus, who hugged her

around the neck. I lifted the saddle skirt, and there were the initials *C.M.* "Take a look," I said to Hackmann. "Questions get asked, you best remember." I paused and fixed him with a warning glare. "Or I'll be back to see you."

He nodded hastily, a sheen of perspiration on his greasy face despite the chill in the air. He indicated the two bushwhackers sprawled in the mud. "What— what about them?"

"The boy here gets what's his. Rest you keep for the trouble of burying them."

He raised his eyebrows. "Fair enough."

I suppressed a cynical grin. He was blasted well right it was fair enough, seeing as soon as we were out of sight he'd dump the two bodies in the river. I nodded to Cyrus. "Find what is yours and your Pa's. Leave the rest."

Cyrus quickly rummaged through the gear. "Looks like most of it's here."

"Your pa have any cash on him?"

"I reckon. Don't know how much. He kept it in a brown wallet."

To no one's surprise, the wallet turned up in the fat man's coat pocket. I tossed it to Cyrus and gestured to the bedroll tied to the cantle of the saddle. "If I was you, I'd leave the bedroll behind. Considering the kind of trash he was, it's probably full of lice." I turned to face Hackmann, the Henry still cradled in my arm and pointing just off to his left. "I reckon since you're taking possession of these old boys' hardware and the horse and saddle, you could afford to toss in a couple clean blankets and a new tarp."

Hackmann nodded so fast his fat cheeks shook like jelly. "Yes, sir. I sure reckon I can."

Chapter Nine

We headed downriver. From what I picked up from Hackmann, the next village down the trace was Milam. After Milam was Sabinetown, which was on the river. That's where I figured we'd head.

Fortunately, the drunken traveler who first blazed the circuitous road from Round Bend Landing to Hackmann's had sobered up when he started for Milam and Sabinetown. He observed the old saying that "the shortest distance between two points is a straight line."

Around noon, we pulled up to the edge of one of the many sloughs along the river. While I built a fire and put coffee on to boil, Cyrus declared he would catch us some fish for that night's supper. I just shook my head and chalked it up to the enthusiasm of youth.

"I put out four lines," he announced upon his return.

While we chewed on cold venison and sipped coffee, he kept his eyes on the lines. Just before we finished, he jumped up and raced around the shore of the slough.

Two of his lines were jerking.

Before I could say a word, he pulled in two fat catfish, each around four or five pounds. I leaned back and shook my head. That Cyrus boy was some youngster.

We made a snug camp that night, far off the road in the middle of a wild thicket. We enjoyed hot coffee, flat biscuits, and broiled filets of flaky white catfish.

Later, as we lay in our soogans staring at the starry heavens above, I proposed my plan to him. "When we reach Milam, I'll put you on the road to Nacogdoches. About ten miles before you hit town is the Bar H. The owner is Stillman Hopkins. He's got a boy about my age, Arch, and a daughter, Mary Catherine. You can stay there until we decide what's best for you."

Personally, I figured the idea was a fairly sound one, far removed from some of my more questionable ideas. That's why I was so surprised when he replied, "I'm going with you."

So convinced was I of the indisputable wisdom of my suggestion that I thought I'd misunderstood him. "Do what?"

"I said I'm going with you."

I sat up and shot him a warning look. "You are not going with me. I'm not sure I can do what I've got to do just looking after myself. I don't need another body to worry over."

He rolled over and looked at me defiantly. "You don't have to worry about me. I can take care of myself."

For several moments, we locked eyes. "If you won't do it on your own, I'll turn you over to the sheriff in Milam. He'll see that you stay put." My eyes dared him to argue.

Lowering his eyes, he replied somberly, "Don't reckon I'd have a choice like that."

I grinned in smug satisfaction, but the grin turned into a frown when he looked up at me and grinned. "But as soon as he looked the other way, I'd follow."

All I could do was shake my head. "I ought to yank you over my knee and whale the daylights out of you, you hard-headed little sprout."

He shrugged. "Wouldn't do no good. I'd still follow."

With a loud exclamation of disgust, I lay back and squeezed my eyes shut. Seemed like every time I thought I might be closing in on those I sought, something stepped in the way. Angrily, I yanked the blankets up around my neck and turned on my side, my back to Cyrus.

I couldn't sleep. I kept remembering what it was like to be sixteen and an orphan. At least I'd had William. Cyrus had nobody. And in all honesty, I couldn't blame him for his feelings.

But, blast it all, none of this was fair to me.

On the other hand, Jedidiah, I said to myself, most of the hands you been forced to play have been unfair.

Next morning, the silence surrounding breakfast was filled with tension. While we were saddling up, I cleared my throat. "I reckon if you got so much store set on riding along with me, I guess you might as well. Just try not to cause me no trouble."

He remained silent. I gave him a sidelong glance as I swung into the saddle. He had a grin on his face as wide as the Sabine River.

The steamship *Captain Howard* was still ahead of us when we reached Sabinetown, so we were forced to continue our journey downriver. We traveled hard, and we traveled long. Not once did Cyrus complain. Him and that sorrel remained right at my side.

We had no better luck at Burkeville, nor Newton, nor Salem's Landing.

Finally, at Madison, a small town a few miles north of the confluence of the Sabine and Neches Rivers, I found the *Captain Howard*. It had been in dock two days. Berthed next to it was a small clipper, the *Queen Anne*.

I left Cyrus with our ponies at dockside as I went aboard. The captain eyed me with distaste, and I didn't much blame him. I reckoned I did look like I'd been ground up and put away wet. But, despite my appearance, the captain was a polite and gracious man.

"Sorry, Mister Walker. I don't recollect the gent."

He held up his hand. "Maybe my bosun will." He leaned out the window and gave a shout.

I found out later that a bosun is like a ranch foreman. He's the one that gives the orders and kicks the rumps. The bosun was named Benoit, and he spoke with a funny accent, almost how I figured someone talking French would sound. "*Oui*, Captain. De steward, he tell me dis little man, he stay in his room. He never come out. Like he be scared of something."

The captain glanced at me, then said, "Any idea where he headed from here?"

"No, Captain. I see dis one when he go ashore, but I pays no mind to where he go."

Ashore, I went directly to the steamship office with Cyrus in tow. I described Abner, but the clerk didn't remember him.

Back on our ponies, Cyrus looked up at me. "Now what?"

I studied the small, dilapidated village around us. "Well, there's two of us. You ask at the stores. I'll take the rough places. Maybe between us, we'll pick up a stroke of luck."

Truth was, I didn't believe my own words, but then, what choice did I have?

As I came out of the third saloon, Cyrus came running up to me. "Jed! Jed, come quick. I found him!"

He spun and raced back up the muddy street to the dock. "There," he said, pointing to the small clipper that was pulling away from the dock.

I sprinted after him, my hopes surging. "Where?"

"Standing by the side. See him?"

By the rail stood a thin hombre, short, and he was wearing a black slicker, but the distance was too far to discern his features. I fought against the sense of disappointment washing over me.

Cyrus face was lit with elation. "Was that him, Jed? Huh?"

"I don't rightly know, boy. I couldn't get a good look at him."

"But, he was small, and he was wearing a black slicker."

"Yep." I forced a grin and laid my hand on his shoulder. "I reckon he is. You done good, Cyrus, real good."

He must have sensed the disappointment in my voice, for a frown knit his forehead. "But, he might not be the one, huh?"

I glanced back at the steamship office. I had an idea. "Let's find out."

Back in the office, the clerk recognized me. Before he could say a word, I said, "You the only one who sells tickets?"

"Huh? Oh. Oh, why, no."

Cyrus grinned.

"This other jasper who sells tickets. Where can I find him?"

"Why—he's indisposed right now."

I frowned. "What do you mean, indisposed?"

He shrugged. "Unavailable. Can't see you."

My frown deepened. "Why not? He ain't sleeping or anything. It's the middle of the day."

The clerk stammered, so I decided to help him make up his mind. "I don't want no trouble, friend, but I promise I'll indispose you right out into the middle of that river if you don't tell me where this feller is."

His face paled. He stammered some more and pointed across the street. Finally, he managed to stutter, "At—at the Bulldog Saloon, eating dinner. Name's Green, J-Jacob Green."

I touched the tip of my finger to my brim. "Much obliged, friend."

Jake Green was as convivial as his co-worker was unfriendly. "Sure enough I remember the little feller," he said, slapping slabs of beef and cheese on a thick slice of bread until he had a sandwich three inches thick. "Sold him a ticket on the *Queen Anne*."

I couldn't help but notice Cyrus eyeing the platter of cold cuts, cheese, onions, pickles, and boiled eggs on the bar for the drinking patrons. I had a couple dollars left, so I ordered me a beer and Cyrus a sarsaparilla and pointed him at the cold cuts.

He didn't waste any time.

Green laughed. "Your boy looks like he ain't eaten nothing in a month."

I sipped my beer. "How come you remember this man?"

He took a huge bite of his sandwich, and while he was chewing, managed to mumble, "Hard not to. It weren't his size, but the fact he was missing a little finger. You know how unusual that is? I mean, losing a little finger. Take a look around. Most fellers who lose fingers lose the first or second. It ain't often you see either of the last two gone."

"Whereabouts the ship heading?"

"Galveston. Then on down the coast to Tampico."

I drained my beer. "How long to Galveston?"

"A couple days. Weather ain't bad. Yeah, a couple days."

Cyrus had already put himself around one sandwich and was starting on a second. If he could handle a third, he'd better get with it, I told myself. He'll sure need it. "When we rode into town, Mister Green, I spotted some railroad tracks heading east. Are there any around heading west?"

"Not here in Madison," he replied, taking another large bite. "Over to Beaumont. Tracks there go to Houston and Galveston."

I pushed back from the table. "Where's the road to Beaumont?" I asked while building my own sandwich.

He pointed with his sandwich. "Follow the street right out of town."

The road from Madison to Beaumont cut across the coastal prairie, a flat, overgrown expanse of vegetation growing in what seemed like three inches of soil on top of a foot of water. Our camp was miserable that night. We reached Beaumont around noon.

"How we going to pay for train tickets, Jed?"

I shook my head. "Don't plan on it. All I know

about the country around here is that it's muddy and there's a heap of rivers and lakes. The railroad people have already cut across the mud and water. We'll just ride along their tracks."

We reached Galveston in three days. The city bustled with life. Its population of almost 14,000 made it the largest city in Texas.

We were worn to a nub. Our horses were exhausted, our gear was wearing thin, and our duds were only a stiff wind away from blowing off our lanky frames. We had twenty-one dollars between us: my one and the twenty Cyrus had found in his pa's wallet.

The first stop we made in Galveston was the dock, where we discovered the *Queen Anne* moored and deserted.

I stood on the dock, studying the city before me. Finding Abner or Scarnose among the dives and dens of Galveston would be like finding a particular tick on a grizzly's back, remote and dangerous.

There was no choice.

We stabled our ponies and for an extra dollar the liveryman let us throw our soogans in the loft. "We could be here quite a spell," I told Cyrus. "So we've got to get work to take care of us."

Cyrus was more than willing. The liveryman hired him to feed and groom the animals as well as keep the place clean. For that, we could sleep in the loft at no charge. I found a job swamping out the Jolly Roger Saloon, two dollars a day for meals. A dollar seventy-five if Cyrus ate. That was fine with me. In fact, I kind of felt sorry for my boss because the way that boy put grub down his gullet, a quarter wouldn't take care of the first bite.

But I stopped feeling guilty after the first few days, when I learned the profit my boss made on the watered-down whiskey and cheap beer.

In our spare time, we began our search, beginning with the area around the livery and spreading in every direction. We took a four-block section at a time, going into every business twice a day, every day for three days, then moving on. We traveled on foot, figuring we could fit into the anonymity of the crowd easier that way than by riding horseback.

"This will certain take a long time, Jed," Cyrus whispered one night in the loft as we climbed into our soogans.

He was right. "I know."

There was silence. Only the distant shouts and laughter from the saloons echoed through the night.

"Jed?"

"Yeah?"

"How long you been looking?"

"Twelve years."

He whistled softly.

"And all that time, you ain't never had a home?"

I drew a deep breath. "No, boy. I don't reckon I have."

Another several seconds of silence passed, then Cyrus whispered, "I'm sorry, Jed."

I stared at the darkness over my head. I could feel tears pooling in my eyes. I was sorry too. And I thought of the Bar H.

Chapter Ten

The first few days in Galveston we focused our search on the underbelly of the city: the slums, the crumbling tenements, the pestholes that infected the darker side of city life.

I insisted that Cyrus be back in the livery each day before sundown. The narrow streets teemed with brigands and thieves who would cut a throat for two bits.

My job ended at midnight, even though the saloon remained open twenty-four hours a day. Several nights, as I made my way along the dark alleys and narrow streets to the livery, I was confronted by over-eager thieves and muggers, whom I sent scrabbling into the surrounding darkness with my Colt.

One night, I climbed into the loft and discovered Cyrus gone. I clambered back down the ladder and quickly searched the livery, cursing under my breath. He was nowhere to be found.

As I turned to go out into the night, he appeared, a sheepish grin on his face.

"Oh. Hi, Jed," he mumbled, trying to appear nonchalant, but failing miserably.

"Where the sam hill you been?" I glared at him, my fists jammed into my hips. "You know how dangerous it is out there?"

He shrugged. "Sorry. I lost track of time."

I stared at him, uncertain I understood what he was saying. "Lost track of time?" I gestured beyond the livery. "You mean you were out this time of night looking for Scarnose?"

He grimaced and seemed to draw back within himself. "Well, it's not as dangerous as you think. Honest."

I snorted. "Don't tell me that, boy. I know how dangerous it is out there." I jabbed a finger at his chest. "I might not be your pa, but I'm telling you true that next time that you pull that kind of stunt, I'll whale the daylights out of you."

He chewed on his lip and nodded. "I won't. I promise."

"And you'd better not forget that either." I glared at him a moment longer, then hooked my thumb over my shoulder. "Now, get up to bed."

After a month of searching, we had seen neither hide nor hair of Scarnose or Abner. I was beginning to believe that I'd missed again, that neither hombre was in Galveston.

The older I grow, the more life forces me to believe in fate, for about the time I thought I had lost the two of them, I spotted Abner.

One night, I had just swept the saloon floor for the last time and had paused in the back door with a trash can in either hand when Abner entered the saloon through the front door. Hastily, I stepped out into the darkness and set the trash cans on the ground next to the saloon. Moving quickly, I hurried down the alley and circled the block so I could watch the front door of the saloon.

Fifteen minutes later, Abner came out and turned down the dimly lit street. A fog had settled in. The sidewalks and brick streets shone in the flickering candlelight cast by the lamps lighting the streets.

Only a handful of late-night revelers were on the sidewalks. Abner made no effort to hurry. I grinned. Occasionally, he glanced over his shoulder, but maintained his casual, almost lazy saunter. Ten minutes later, he entered the Dark Horse Saloon.

I edged up to the door and peered through the foggy glass. A dozen or so patrons sat at a handful of tables. Beyond, Abner was heading up the stairs to the mezzanine on the second floor. Pulling my hat down over my eyes, I quickly followed.

On the mezzanine, I spotted a door closing down the hall. I glanced over the rail at the men below. No one was paying me any attention, so I eased closer to the wall and shucked my sixgun.

Staying on the balls of my feet, I slipped down the hall. Just before I reached the door, it opened and Abner stepped out. Behind him came Scarnose.

Abner spotted me.

"Back," the small man shouted, lunging backward and knocking Scarnose back into the room. He slammed the door, and as I leaped forward, I heard the deadbolt slam home.

Cursing, I threw my shoulder into the door. It groaned. From inside came the sound of a breaking window. I backed off and lunged at the door again. This time, it cracked. Muttered oaths came from under the door, along with the sound of more breaking glass.

I clenched my teeth and hurled my body into door. With a splitting crack, it burst from the hinges and slammed to the floor. I raced to the window and peered out in time to see the two of them scrambling down a ladder.

A surge of adrenaline coursed through my veins, pumping fresh and revitalizing oxygen to my muscles. In one leap, I hit the ladder and bounded down, leaping from the third rung to the ground and racing after the two men as they disappeared into the fog down the dark alley.

They turned up a narrow street near the livery and disappeared through a darkened doorway. Just before I reached the door, a shadow stepped out, followed by five or six others.

I slid to a halt as they passed under the streetlight. Judging by their garb, they were sailors, a ragtag collection of buccaneers, scullers, and roustabouts, the dregs of the earth who make up the lowest echelon in the ship's crew. The flickering candlelight illuminated the weapons clutched in their knobby fists, belaying pins and knives, weapons to crush and slash. One stepped forward with a sixgun in his hand. "You come far enough, mate. Time for you to meet with Davy Jones."

"I wouldn't count on it, friend," I replied, cocking my Colt and taking a step backward.

As one, the sailors stepped forward.

I drew a deep breath, wondering what my chances were of outrunning them.

Suddenly, I heard a whisper. "Pssst. Jed, back here."

It was Cyrus.

I glanced over my shoulder into a darkened doorway. "In here," he whispered urgently. "Hurry."

Without hesitation, I jumped through the door. He slammed it behind me, then grabbed my hand. "Follow me, and keep your head down."

Where we were heading, I had no idea. All I knew was that it had to be better than where I was.

Abruptly, Cyrus stopped. I could hear him groping along the wall. I put out one hand and touched cold, damp bricks. I had the feeling we were in a narrow tunnel. I lifted my arm and touched the ceiling, a foot or so above my head.

He whispered, "Just a minute." Seconds later, a match flared, and he lit a small candle. "We have to hurry, but be careful here." He held the candle down to the floor, revealing a wide plank spanning a dark hole. "We cross here. I'll go first, then light the way for you."

Behind us came the muffled sound of curses and shuffling of feet. Slowly, Cyrus eased across, then turned back to me. I eyed the plank skeptically. It spanned a six-foot opening from which I could hear lapping waves below. Gingerly, I stepped on the board. As I put my weight on it, it sagged.

"Move as fast as you can," Cyrus whispered. "You don't want the board to break."

That was one warning he didn't have to give. Two seconds later, I was on his side. He quickly slid the board from the hole and backed away several feet, where he placed the candle on the floor. He grinned up at me. "When they see the candle, they'll move faster. They won't pay attention to the hole." He turned on his heel, lighting a second candle as he did. "Now let's go."

"How deep is that hole?"

He replied as he hurried along the narrow tunnel, "Fifteen or twenty feet. Best I could figure, the bay water is below us. I figure this is how the old pirates came in and out."

A few minutes later, terrified screams echoed from the darkness behind us. Cyrus giggled. "Looks like they found the hole. Okay, we're at the end of the tunnel. We're under the dock. We have to jump in and swim from here," he said. "Just to the ladder out there."

Ten or fifteen feet distant, I spotted the silhouette of a ladder to the top of the pier.

"Don't wait for me," I said, jumping into the icy water and heading for the ladder.

Ten minutes later, we reached the livery.

As we changed out of our wet duds, I studied the young boy. "I should tan your rear for going out again when I told you not to, but I wouldn't have my heart in it since you sure saved my bacon back there."

He grinned. "Those little passages are everywhere under the town. And hardly nobody uses them. I don't reckon very many folks even know about them."

"How'd you find them?"

He shrugged. "I just kinda stumbled on them," he replied. "The first time was . . ."

He spent the next ten minutes relating how he discovered and explored the passages. For the most part, they led into saloons and general stores. "I suppose maybe pirates used them to sneak in and out of town, don't you, Jed?"

"Makes sense," I replied, studying the youngster who was turning out to be not only a hard worker, but also a bright young man. "Now, let's get to sleep. We got us a heap of looking to do tomorrow."

We were on the streets early the next morning, starting with the one that ran in front of the Dark Horse

Saloon. A light fog lay over the town, reflecting the morning sun in a surreal glow.

By mid-morning, the fog had burned off and a bright March sun beat down on the town. Having no luck, we headed back to the livery at noon, stopping off at Maceo's General Store for crackers, tins of sardines, and peaches.

From the loft, we studied the schooners and clippers loading at the dock while we ate. His blond hair hanging almost to his shoulders, Cyrus looked up at me. "Where do you suppose they're going?"

"Your guess is as good as mine. Around the world, I reckon."

His face got all dreamy. "Sure would be something to see all them tropical islands with all the natives running around."

I chuckled. "Well, boy, one thing certain, it would sure be something diffe—" I froze, staring at two figures walking across the dock about a quarter of a mile distant. One was small, about the stature of Abner. "Stay here," I said, jumping to my feet and dropping my dinner on the floor.

Cyrus looked around fearfully. "What is it?"

"Just do what I said. Stay here." I climbed down the ladder and hurried from the livery, keeping my eyes on the two jaspers heading for a small clipper. From time to time, they glanced over their shoulders. When they did, I'd look down, or glance away, or head in a different direction.

As I drew closer, I recognized Abner. My heart thudded against my chest. I walked faster, but before I could get close enough, they climbed the gangplank of the small clipper and disappeared into the cabins.

I stopped beside some crates labeled JAPANESE SILK that were bound for Houston and Austin. There was only one way off the ship. Unless, I reminded myself, they were on to stay. If I saw the ship was making ready to leave and the two were still aboard, then I'd simply have to go aboard myself.

Thirty minutes later, Cyrus came up behind me. "What are you looking at, Jed?"

I nodded toward the ship. "They're aboard."

His eyes grew wide. "Can I help?"

Keeping my eyes on the stevedores loading the ship, I shook my head. "Nothing you can do, Cyrus. But you can find you a place to duck when the shooting starts."

"Shooting?"

I laughed bitterly. "I sure don't plan on shaking hands with those two jaspers."

Time dragged.

The wind shifted to the north and the light breeze carried a chill. Suddenly, I stiffened. Abner and a second man appeared on deck. The distance was too far to discern a scar. I had to wait. I shucked my Colt and whispered over my shoulder, "Find a place to hide, Cyrus."

The two descended the gangplank. I eased farther

back until only a slice of my head peered around the corner of the crate of silks.

Abner wore western garb, but the second man was dressed as a sailor, with wide-legged pants, a black heavy sweater pulled up around his neck, an unbuttoned pea coat, and woolen watch cap.

They headed directly toward me. I flexed my fingers around the butt of my Colt. Twelve years I had waited for this moment; twelve long, painful years.

They grew closer. Holding the Colt behind my back, I lowered my head and started toward them. I heard their footsteps. Just before we reached each other, I stepped in their path and pulled the Colt down on them. "Hold it right there." My eyes went instantly to the taller man. A cold hand squeezed my heart when I spotted the scar across the bridge of his nose.

Abner's eyes grew wide when he spotted the six-gun.

Scarnose just glared at me with narrow-set eyes. He growled, "What's this all about, cowboy?"

"He's the one I told you about, Darby," said Abner. "The hombre asking them questions in the saloon about you."

"Shut up, Abner." Darby threw his shoulders back and jammed his thumbs behind his belt. "I asked you what this was all about, cowboy."

"Twelve years, Darby. That's what it's all about."

His large broad forehead wrinkled in a frown. "Twelve years?" He shook his head. "I got no idea what you're talking about."

"Then I'll tell you. I always believed a man should know why he's going to die."

Abner took a deep step back. Darby glanced to either side and ran his tongue over his lips. "I don't know you. Why should you kill me?"

I spat out the answer. "Because you shot me and killed my brother."

He looked at me in disbelief. "You? Why, I ain't never seen you."

Abner nodded his agreement emphatically.

In a calm, steady voice, I said, "Twelve years ago in Missouri. You and four others bushwhacked my brother and me and stole our herd of cattle. I've taken care of two of your boys. Now, I got you two."

A look of recognition came into his eyes, but he tried to bluster his way out. "Missouri? I ain't never been there."

I nodded. "Don't turn yellow on me now, Darby. The last thing I remember before passing out is that scar on your nose. There's no mistaking that."

He snorted. "Bull. I never been there, I tell you." He put out his arm to brush my gun hand aside. "Now, I got business. I ain't got time to listen to you."

I stepped forward and jammed the muzzle of the Colt into his hard belly. "You're right about one thing, Darby. You ain't got no time left."

Behind me, Cyrus shouted, "Jed! Look out!"

My head exploded in a blinding blast of pain.

As I fell to the ground, the last words I heard were "Grab the boy."

Chapter Eleven

Deep in the darkness around me, I became aware of a rolling, undulating motion. Then a slight throbbing started in the back of my head, intensifying into the pounding of a blacksmith's hammer as I eased back into consciousness.

I opened one eye and stared into the curious eyes of a rat, which instantly squeaked and darted into the darkness. I opened my other eye and stared at a large coil of manila hawsers. I tried to move, but my hands and feet were bound.

Closing my eyes against the pounding in my skull, I tried to relax and collect my thoughts. The rolling movement of the deck at my back told me I was on a ship, but headed for where? Light seeped through cracks in the wall, so I figured it was still day.

My head seemed filled with a fuzzy haze through

which several disjointed thoughts tumbled. Slowly I fit some into place. I remembered confronting Abner and Scarnose. Then the blow to my head.

I stiffened, remembering the last words I heard before I slipped into unconsciousness. "Grab the boy." I stared into the gloom over my head. Cyrus! I craned my neck to peer into the shadows about me. I relaxed. He wasn't here. Maybe he'd escaped.

Suddenly, the door swung open and a lantern blinded me. I closed my eyes, but when I heard a cruel laugh, I opened them again and spotted Abner's sneering face above the lantern.

"Well, well. Look who's awake." He stood hipshot, staring down at me, his thin lips curled in amusement.

I glared at him.

"You're one of them tough ones, huh? Won't say nothing?" He grunted. "Thought you had us back there, huh? Shoot, it'll take a jasper a heap smarter than you to run us down. But you ain't going to get another chance. Tonight, you're going to fall overboard. That'll fix your bacon. And with a hundred pounds of chain tied around you, you sure ain't going to do no swimming." He laughed and closed the door.

I lay motionless, my brain racing, wondering how much time I had left to figure out something, anything. I looked around the small room in which I was confined. A storage room. First thing was to free myself from these ropes, and then I could figure out my next step.

I rolled into a sitting position and drew my legs

back toward me. I prayed that they hadn't found the knife I kept in my boot. My fingers touched the reassuring handle of the blade.

Quickly, I sawed through my bonds. When the ropes fell away, I clambered to my feet, knife in hand. I pressed an eye to one of the cracks and peered into the cabin. It appeared deserted. I eased the door open and stepped out into the empty room. Shadows were deepening as night drew near. From far away, a roll of thunder reverberated through the beams of the ship.

I studied the room. There were two bunks in the room, so I guessed it was where two of the junior officers slept.

Against one bulkhead was a desk, which I quickly searched. I grinned when I found a Navy Colt and a box of cartridges in the bottom drawer.

"Thank you, Mister Colt," I whispered while checking the cylinder.

Through the porthole, I saw the blood-red glow of the setting sun splash over the beach several hundred yards to the north. Beyond the beach, lightning slashed across a bank of black clouds rolling toward us.

Any time, I told myself, Abner will return. And with help.

I couldn't expect to hold off the entire crew. My only chance was surprise, and to hope in the few moments they were off guard that I could get over the side. I took a deep breath. I hadn't been dealt much of a hand, but I had to play it out.

The rolling of the ship grew more extreme. The seas were building. The whitecaps were growing larger.

Time dragged. Darkness settled in.

I tried to relax in the dark room. My mouth grew dry, and my stomach grew queasy. I closed my eyes and leaned back against the bulkhead, trying to stave off the nausea threatening me.

Growling an acerbic curse, I muttered, "Wouldn't you guess. Of all times to be seasick, I have to pick this one."

Beads of perspiration popped out on my face despite the chill in the cabin. Then I heard the rain against the porthole. Quickly, I stumbled across the undulating floor and threw the porthole open, letting the icy rain pelt against my upturned face.

Suddenly, footsteps sounded outside the door. With the Colt in hand, I pressed up against the bulkhead next to the door. The door swung open and Abner entered, followed by a sailor. "He's right in there," Abner said, lantern in hand, leading the way across the room to the storeroom.

Gently, I closed the cabin door behind the two. "Afraid not."

Both men spun around and froze when they saw the revolver in my hand.

"Nice and easy, boys. Nice and easy." I gestured at the sailor with the muzzle of the Colt. "You. On the floor. And you," I said to Abner, "you put the lantern on the table, then tie and gag him."

When he finished, I motioned him to stand next to

the bulkhead. "W—what are you going to do with me?"

I suppressed the urge to squeeze the trigger. "I should kill you, but that can wait. Right now, you're going to help me out of here."

"Out of here? But how? You're on a ship." A smug grin curled his lips. "You can't escape. There are too many sailors."

"Well, Abner. Just to make you feel better and just so you know where you stand, if I die, you die," I said as I relieved him of his sixgun.

The color drained from his face. He gulped several times, his Adam's apple bobbing up and down like a perch cork.

I buttoned my Mackinaw tight. On a shelf above the desk was a woolen watch cap, which I pulled on. I hoped I could pass for one of them long enough to make my move.

"Land is to the north of us, so that means the ship is heading east. Last I looked out the porthole, I could see land." While I explained what we were going to do, I pulled a Winchester off the gun rack and dropped a box of cartridges in my pocket. "So, you and me are going to go on deck, lower a boat, and head for shore. You must be of some importance to them or they wouldn't have agreed to help you toss me overboard." With a short, sharp gesture of the muzzle, I motioned him to the door. "Move."

* * *

The deck rolled worse than a sunfishing bronco. The cold rain came in gusts, forcing us to lean into it to maintain our footing.

Three sailors were on deck, two at the wheel in the cabin and the other on the bow. We quickly scurried aft into the shadows cast by the cabin. I glanced over my shoulder, hoping the gusting rain sheeting down the cabin windows blurred the wheelman's vision.

Abner hesitated. I jabbed him in the back with the Colt. "Over there. Lower that boat," I said, shoving him toward a small skiff on the port side near the stern. I placed the Winchester in the skiff and glanced at the cabin, halfway expecting one of the wheelmen to be peering through the window at us.

At the same time I kept waiting for shouts of discovery if one of the sailors entered the cabin below and discovered one of their own hogtied.

Abner fumbled with the ropes. I leaned forward. "Hurry or I'll shoot you and swim to shore." I cast a worried glance toward the beach. A flash of lightning lanced across the sky, lighting the shoreline, which I guessed to be a mile or so from us.

I jabbed the muzzle into the small of his back. "I said hurry."

He yanked and fumbled with the lines, finally loosening them. I shoved the skiff beyond the port rail while he lowered it. The wind banged it against the hull.

A head popped out from the cabin. "Hey, what was that?"

"Drop it," I yelled at Abner.

He did, and I shoved him overboard after the skiff. Someone cried out, "Who's out there?"

I fired off two quick shots, sending the seaman scrabbling back into the cabin. I threw myself over the side, splashing deep into the icy water.

As I struggled to the surface, I slid the Colt into my holster and fumbled to hook the rawhide loop over the trigger. I was going to need the sixgun when I reached shore.

Back on the clipper, figures clustered at the rail, shouting into the gusting rain. I spotted the skiff and swam toward it. My heavy coat was weighing me down, but I had a choice of shedding it and freezing when I reached shore, or straining a gut to reach the skiff.

Even a cold beer after a hot day's ride in the summer didn't feel as good as the wet gunwale of the skiff. Holding on to it with one hand, I slipped out of my water-soaked Mackinaw and threw it aboard, clambering in after it.

Lightning flashed, and thunder shook the tiny craft.

By now, the clipper was a few hundred yards away. I looked for Abner, and in the next burst of lightning, I spotted a small head bobbing fifty feet away.

Grabbing the oars, I rowed to him.

Shaking like a half-frozen puppy, he struggled inside and curled up in the stern while I rowed us to shore. The wind seemed to push us back two feet for every one we went forward, but eventually the wooden bow scraped on the sandy shore.

He stood shivering, a scrawny, near helpless excuse for a human. "What do we do now?" he whined. "We'll freeze."

"You might, but I sure as blazes won't. Now, help me haul the skiff back up to the sand dunes. We'll rig up some shelter. Break the wind and keep the rain off."

When we finished, I crawled inside first. Abner dropped to his hands and knees to crawl inside, but I pointed the Winchester at him. "Where you think you're going?"

The darkness hid the expression on his face, but I could imagine his confusion. "What do you mean? I'm coming inside out of the weather."

"No, you aren't. Not until you tell me where I can find Darby."

A flash of lightning lit his stunned features. "You can't do that to me. I'll freeze out here."

I cocked the hammer on the Winchester. "Your choice."

He sat back on his heels and hugged himself forlornly. "That ain't human. That ain't Christian. I'll die out here."

"Only if you want to. Where's Darby?"

He remained silent.

The rain had intensified into sleet.

Abner whined, "It's sleeting."

I stuck my hand out from the shelter. "You know, I think you're right."

He remained on his heels, shivering. Finally, he whispered, "Back in Galveston. He ain't going nowhere. He figures you're dead. Now can I come in?"

Suppressing a grin, I said, "Come on in. Join me. We'll be as snug as a rabbit in his hole."

Well, we might not have been as snug as that rabbit, but we did live to see the sunrise next morning. The rain and sleet had passed, taking the clouds with it. A cold sun fell across a colder marsh.

I crawled out from under the overturned skiff and stretched the cricks and cramps from my muscles. The sharp click of a cocking hammer froze me in place.

"All right, cowboy. Now, it's my turn."

I turned slowly to Abner, who was holding the Winchester pointed at me. I grinned. "Your turn for what?" I nodded to the wild country around us. "You know what's out there? These are the Gulf coast marshes. Alligators the size of a Conestoga wagon prowl those marshes. Water moccasin cottonmouths bigger around than your leg wait at every bend." I shook my head. "You won't get ten feet out there without me, Abner." I gestured to the Winchester. "Put that down, and let's get started."

He stared at me with uncertainty, the defiance slowly fading from his eyes. Finally, he dropped his gaze to the ground and lowered the rifle. "Why didn't you just shoot me instead of bringing me out here to this godforsaken country?"

I studied him for a moment. "I started to, but jail will be worse for you. I'm going to turn you over to the sheriff in Beaumont, but before then, you're going to tell me where I can find Darby and the fifth hombre."

While I had never been in this neck of the woods, I figured if we cut straight across the sprawling prairie of waist-high grass, sooner or later we would intersect either the railroad or a road leading to Beaumont. I had no idea of the distance, but I figured we could find fresh water and food in the marsh. As long as we watched where we put our feet, we would make it through just fine.

Once we reached Beaumont, I'd head back to Galveston.

Traveling was slow through the muck and sludge of the marsh. I didn't tell Abner, but for the most part, alligators and water moccasins hibernated during the winter, so I wasn't too concerned about running into either. On the other hand, I kept my eyes open just in case.

Mid-afternoon, we spotted a motte of stunted oak a quarter mile ahead. The motte, about a hundred feet across, rose above the marsh a few feet. I glanced at Abner. "It's high and dry. I reckon we won't find a better spot for tonight's camp. You go up among those trees and find wood for a fire. I'll get us some supper."

The marsh was teeming with game. Within minutes, I had a fat little rabbit. I dressed him and stuck him on a spit over the fire. While the rabbit roasted, we gathered armloads of slender cane and wove a two-sided windbreaker with a roof.

After the rigors of the last couple days, our rude little shelter seemed like the bridal suite at a fancy hotel. At least it did until the next front blew in around midnight, carrying with it a fresh batch of sleet.

We threw more wood on the fire, but it was obvious we didn't have enough to last until morning. I stumbled out into the storm and staggered through the motte looking for more wood. Suddenly, I spotted lights in the distance.

"What the—" I blinked and rubbed my eyes with my fists. I peered through the sleet. I saw the light again, a dim yellow glow due north of us.

I hurried back to the camp. "Let's go," I said, grabbing the Winchester. "There's a house out there."

We plunged into the marsh, keeping our eyes fixed on the beckoning light.

Abner yelled above the wind. "You sure it's a house?"

"What else?"

Twenty freezing minutes later, we stumbled into a clearing around a small, rude cabin, and banged on the door.

No answer.

We knocked again.

Suddenly, the door jerked open and I stared into the muzzle of a .50 Hawken.

Chapter Twelve

Warily, the bearded settler stepped back and motioned us inside. "Close the door and get over by the fire to warm up," he said, the tone in his voice a clear warning.

Moving slowly, I leaned the Winchester against the wall next to the door before crossing the cluttered room to the small fire in the mudcat hearth to warm my hands. Abner stayed right at my side. "Much obliged, Mister. I was starting to get worried out there," I said over my shoulder.

I glanced at him. He still held the Hawken on us. Beside him was his wife, wrapped in a quilt. Huddling against her were two wide-eyed children, both girls. He eyed us suspiciously. "How come you two is out here?"

I told them the whole story. "Then we spotted your light when we were looking for firewood tonight."

His wife spoke up. "You mean to say you been following after them men all these years?"

"Yes, ma'am." I nodded. "This one I'm taking to jail in Beaumont." I unbuttoned my Mackinaw and pulled it back to reveal my Colt. "If you would feel better, Mister, you can have my sixgun."

He studied me a moment longer, then lowered the Hawken. "No need. Truth is, you old boys can't go no farther than right here without help."

I removed my coat and hung it on a peg in the wall. "How's that?"

"There's only one way out, a shell ridge just under the water. Everywhere else, water's neck deep. No way you can make the twenty miles to Beaumont in neck-deep water in this kind of weather." He gestured to the floor in front of the fireplace. "Reckon you can sleep there. Martha'll get you some quilts."

"Obliged." I nodded to Abner. "This here is Abner. My name's Jed Walker." I stuck out my hand.

He grunted and took my hand. "I'm Wilfred McDade. This here's my wife, Martha, and them two is Liz and Cath."

"Ma'am." I nodded to her.

She smiled shyly in return.

Despite my wet clothes and muddy boots, I had no trouble sleeping. Nor, apparently, did Abner, for he was still snoring when I awoke a few hours later.

Outside, the gray of false dawn filled the sky. The

others were sleeping, so I slipped out and gathered an armload of split firewood, figuring on repaying McDade for his hospitality.

He was up when I returned. A crooked grin spread over his angular face. "Thanks," he said, following me outside, where he headed for the nearby barn.

I took in another armload and dumped it by Abner, jarring him awake. "Come on out to the barn," I said. "Let's give the folks a hand before breakfast."

By now, Mrs. McDade was up and puttering around the pot-bellied stove.

In the barn, we helped feed the animals, and I even milked a cow, something I hadn't done for over twelve years. I noticed that the wall at the end of the barn was only half completed. Beyond lay a stack of logs, probably intended for the express purpose of completing the wall.

Back in the cabin, Mrs. McDade had whipped up a hot breakfast of corn mush, honey, and thick, black coffee.

The table was too small for all of us, so Abner and me squatted by the fire, content to be warm and have something hot to put in our bellies. "I noticed you been working on your barn out there, Mr. McDade."

He and his wife exchanged a quick glance. "Yep. Hadn't done much the last few weeks. Stove up my back. Afraid to take a chance of busting something permanent by hefting any of them logs."

I nodded and shoveled another bite of grub down my gullet. As much as I wanted to get after Darby, I couldn't help admiring these folks who were trying to carve out a place of their own in the middle of a hostile wilderness. "Looking at what you got left to do, Mister McDade, I reckon me and Abner can have that wall the rest of the way up in a couple days. Least we can do for your folks' hospitality."

McDade protested, but I insisted. "Both of us want to, don't we, Abner?" I jabbed him in the side.

He nodded hurriedly. "Yeah. Yeah, we sure do."

Using McDade's old plug horse, we slid the logs in place without a hitch, fit the notches, hammered in the pins, and then plastered the cracks with a thick mixture of mud and grass. By the middle of the second day, we had the job done.

We stepped back to admire our handiwork.

"Boys, I can't tell you how much I appreciate this," said McDade.

"Just glad to help," I said.

Abner grunted. "Yeah."

McDade shook his head. "You deserve something. I got a few dollars put back."

Grinning, I replied, "Another couple meals of your wife's fine cooking will take care of us. I reckon if you don't mind us spending another night, we'll move out in the morning."

That night, before I pulled the quilt up around my neck, I took time to clean mud and salt from the Colt and Winchester. McDade handed me a can of hog lard for grease. He grinned. "Out here, we make do with what we got."

I returned his grin. "This'll do just fine."

During the early morning hours, a blood-curdling scream awakened me. I looked around. The light cast by the small fire in the hearth was dim, but not too dim that I couldn't see that Abner was missing.

Suddenly, the door burst open and the thin man rushed in, holding his neck and screaming. "Help me! Please, help."

By now, everyone was awake. I hurried to him while McDade lit the lantern. "What is it?" I yelled at the screaming man.

"Snakebite. A snake bit me." His legs gave way, and he sat heavily on the floor.

Outside, hogs squealed.

I knelt and pulled Abner's hand away from his neck. Two holes an inch and a half apart on the side of his neck glistened with blood and poison.

He gasped for breath, and his eyes fluttered shut. He opened them wide and stared at me. "Hurry. Do something. Please, do something. I feel funny," Abner begged, beginning to cry.

"Let me look," Mrs. McDade said, pushing my hand aside. Gently, she wiped at the blood with a rag. She glanced up at her husband and shook her head.

Abruptly, the hogs stopped squealing.

Abner grabbed my arm. "Please, you got to help. This is all your fault." His voice grew fainter. He slurred his words. "You—should have—have—left me . . ." His eyelids rolled down, and he slumped back on the floor.

We stared at him several moments.

"Snakebit." McDade shook his head. "Ain't too many out this time of year. Wonder where he was."

The two girls, Liz and Cath, stood beside their mother, wide-eyed at the scene before them. Looking at them, I remembered McDade mentioning the day before that he had a few dollars put away. "You mentioned you had a few dollars put back." I looked around the small cabin. "You keep it in here?"

McDade and his wife exchanged looks. "No." The man shook his head. "Did once, but while we were over at Sabinetown, someone stole it. I hide it out under the hog trough." He chuckled. "I built that trough a few inches off the ground so it wouldn't rot so fast. I figured no one would look in the hog pen. Besides, sometimes snakes crawl under it to stay warm, if the hogs don't get them first."

I pondered the facts. "How do you reckon he found out about the hiding spot?"

McDade shook his head. "Don't see how. Only me and the wife know about it."

"What about the girls?"

"You know how nosy kids are. If we'd told them, they'd have to see for themselves, and we don't want them out there at all because of the snakes and hogs."

I reached for the lantern. "Abner was bleeding right good. Let's find out where this all came about."

With the lantern in one hand and the sixgun in the other, we followed the trail of blood straight to the hog pen. We didn't have to go any farther. In the middle of the pen, a boar hog was chewing on a fat cottonmouth.

McDade whistled softly. "So that's what happened." He frowned up at me. "But how did he find out?"

"If you said nothing, and if your wife said nothing, then that leaves the girls."

"But they don't know nothing about the money."

"Let's see what we can find out," I replied, heading back to the house.

The answer was waiting for us. Martha McDade spoke as soon as we came in. The two girls clung to their mother. "The girls told him about the hog pen." She hugged them to her. "They said he asked them about the money last night. When they told him they didn't know nothing, he asked if there was some place their Pa told them to never go. They told him the hog pen."

"What?" McDade exclaimed.

"That's what they told me."

Grimacing, I shook my head. "Looks like Abner was too clever for his own good."

"I don't understand," McDade said.

"Abner was a thief and a killer. He was the kind that tried to read between the lines, who was so used to lying that he figured everyone did. So, if someone said one thing, he might have figured it meant something else. I'm betting that he figured you told the girls not to go around the hog pen because if they did, they might find the money."

McDade eyed me skeptically.

With a shrug, I nodded to the girls. "Where else have you told them not to go?"

He pointed outside. "The marsh. The marsh and the hog pen. As long as they stay away from those two places, they'll be just fine."

I knelt in front of the girls and smiled at them. "When Abner asked you where you couldn't go, what did you tell him?"

The two exchanged looks, then Liz blurted out, "Just what Papa always says, for us not to go into the marsh or the hog pen."

I looked over my shoulder. "He figured you wouldn't hide it out in the marsh. If you hid the money, it would be around here. And," I added, "he was right."

McDade stared down at the motionless body. "Poor jasper. Never figured on the snake."

Later that morning, with a bag of grub over my shoulder and the Winchester in my hand, I pulled out for Beaumont. McDade took me several hundred yards into the marsh and then pointed out the shell ridge. He gave me a six-foot pole. "The ridge is about ten feet or so wide." He pointed above the head-high cane. "It goes straight for a couple miles, then angles back to the right. Another few miles, and you run into the

Sabinetown and Aurora road. Aurora's to the left. You can get to Beaumont from Aurora."

We shook hands. "Good luck, Mister McDade," I said.

"Good luck to you, Mister Walker."

Some years later, I heard that McDade had discovered pirate treasure buried on the beach, maybe where Abner and me had washed ashore. He hauled it to his place and buried it. On the way to New Orleans to sell cattle, he died.

His wife, Martha, had paid no attention when he buried the treasure, and, so the story went, she never found it.

I couldn't help wondering if she looked under the hog trough.

Two days of hard travel put me in Beaumont. I was bone-weary and footsore. My duds were rags, and I was broke. I looked at the Winchester I carried, figuring I could get a few dollars for it.

To my surprise, when I headed down the main street toward the railroad, I spotted a figure riding toward me, trailing a familiar-looking dun horse. Then I recognized Cyrus.

Chapter Thirteen

Cyrus was as surprised to see me as I was him. He jumped from his pony and rushed to me. "Jed!" He threw out his arms, but stopped just before he reached me. I guess he figured he was too grownup to be hugging another man, so he stuck out his hand. "It sure is good to see you."

I shook his hand vigorously. "Boy, you're sure a sight for sore eyes. How come you're over here and not back in Galveston?"

He pointed east, toward Madison. "I've been following Darby."

My hopes soared. "Darby?"

"Yes. I got away from them when they knocked you out. I hid and then followed him back to his room. A couple days later, he rode out, and I followed." His face glowed with excitement. "And look," he blurted out, pointing at the dun. "I brought your horse and gear."

I took another look at Cyrus. He was turning into a fairly responsible young man. I nodded and walked over to the dun. While I rubbed his neck, I asked Cyrus, "What made you think to bring him with you?"

He shrugged. "I don't know. I reckon I figured that I'd run across you sooner or later."

I grinned when I spotted my Yellowboy Henry in the boot. I slipped the Winchester under the saddle fender and snugged it to the cinch rings with the leather strings, and then I swung aboard. "How much later was you willing to wait?"

Cyrus climbed into his saddle. He looked me square in the eyes. "I reckon as long as it took."

I studied him a few moments. It felt good knowing at least one person thought of me like kin.

The Winchester brought a few dollars, enough for clean duds and a solid meal for the two of us. Between bites of steak, I asked Cyrus, "How did you find out Darby was going to Madison?"

His eyes lit with mischief. "You know all them secret passages back in Galveston?"

"Yeah."

"Well, there was one that opened into Darby's room. He didn't know nothing about it, so I hid there sometimes. That's how I found out he was going to Madison. He's supposed to meet some jasper named Suggs at one of the saloons."

I washed the steak down with a slug of coffee. "How far ahead of us is he?"

"Not far. Half a day, I'd guess. I been just trailing along easy like. If I spotted something ahead, I'd drop back."

I studied him several seconds. "You been playing a dangerous game, boy. You know it?"

He gave me a crooked grin. "Yes, but you'd do the same for me."

He was right there. I grinned. "Okay, then, partner. Let's rustle our spurs out of here."

We reached Madison just after sunset the next day. We pulled up at the edge of town. Gaudy lights sparkled up and down the street. Tinny music poured out of the saloons, and raucous laughter echoed along the board sidewalks.

Cyrus looked up at me. "Where first?"

I nodded to his side of the street. "We know what he looks like. You take that side. I'll take this. Don't let him see you. I want to get him by himself to get that last name out of him."

The main street was only a quarter of a mile long, but it had more saloons jammed in it than wind in a bull turned loose in a patch of green corn. Mixed in with the saloons were tonsorial parlors, bathing facilities, general stores, and a single dress shop for the ladies.

We covered both sides of the street, but Darby was nowhere around.

Cyrus looked up at me hopefully. "Maybe he hasn't got here yet."

"No. I'm betting he's here. I'm just wondering if he's already met this Suggs hombre and rode out." I studied the town, trying to decide where I would go if I were Darby.

Cyrus pointed to the Cattleman Hotel across the street. "You think he might be over there?"

I shrugged. "Hard to say. We start asking questions, then we might draw attention to ourselves."

The young boy persisted. "Yeah, but if he's already been here and gone, then we won't have to waste any time around here. We can get on his trail."

I had to admit his argument made sense.

He started toward the hotel. "Hold on," I called after him. "Where do you think you're going?"

"The hotel. The clerk won't think nothing about a kid asking for someone. Don't worry. Nothin'll happen." He turned on his heel and slogged through the mud to the hotel.

Five minutes later, he reappeared and hurried back to me. He shook his head. "They hadn't heard of Darby, but the jasper, Suggs, has a room there." He paused, grinning up at me.

I clapped him on the shoulder. "Cyrus, you done good."

We hung around the saloons until after midnight, but no sign of Darby. We stabled our ponies in the livery and slept in the stalls with them.

Next morning, we rose early, tended our ponies,

saddled up, and led our horses outside. We tied them to the rail in front of the livery.

The streets were almost deserted, populated by sleepy merchants opening their shops, the hog reeve chasing the hogs off the main street, and a few stevedores loading last-minute goods aboard the *Captain Howard* steamboat for its journey upstream.

By eight o'clock, the streets teemed with business. Wagons of every style splashed through the streets: Morgans, lumber wagons, buckboards. Lumbermen stomped the mud from their spiked boots as they stalked into the saloons. Refined ladies in skirts and dart-fitted bodices scurried down the boardwalks, ignoring the naughty taunts cast at them by the crib girls on the balconies.

Like the night before, Cyrus took one side of the street and I took the other.

I found Darby in the fourth saloon. He sat at a back table with a surly-looking hombre with broad shoulders and a mashed-in face that looked like it had been arranged by the underside of a horse's hoof.

Stepping to the edge of the boardwalk, I whistled to Cyrus and motioned for him to bring our horses up. He nodded and hurried to our ponies. I went back to the batwing doors and peered over the top.

The saloon was filled with smoke and riotous shouts and laughter. An off-key piano banged out an unrecognizable tune. Keeping my eyes on Darby, I shucked the Colt and gave the cylinder a spin, checking the action. It spun easily, emitting a series of purring clicks. I grinned when I remembered the hog lard McDade had given me to lubricate the sixgun. I gave the cylinder another spin and nodded my head. Hog lard or not, it worked. I holstered the revolver and waited.

Cyrus pulled up in front of the general store next to the saloon. He remained in his saddle, holding the dun's reins in his hand.

Down the street at the dock, the *Captain Howard* sounded its whistle, a long, wheezing bellow that echoed up and down the swift brown waters of the Sabine. I reckoned they were making ready to shove off.

Inside, Darby and Suggs pushed back from the table and headed for the door. Darby wore two side guns high on his waist. From the way Suggs wore his sixgun low on his leg and tied down, I instantly knew he was a gunnie.

I stepped back, pressing up against the wall next to the door.

Moments later, the two men pushed through the batwing doors and turned toward the docks, their backs to me. "Stop right there, Darby," I growled, cocking the hammer at the same time. "Don't touch those sixguns unless you want a dose of lead poisoning."

Their backs still to me, they held their arms out to the side. "Take it easy, pard," Darby said. "What's this all about?"

"Turn around nice and slow. No fast moves."

Darby's eyes grew wide when he saw me, then narrowed into a malevolent glare. Suggs fixed his small pig eyes on me.

"Surprised, Darby? Probably not half as surprised as Abner was when the cottonmouth got him in the neck." Keeping my eyes on Darby, I spoke to Suggs. "I got nothing on you, cowboy. You want to turn and walk away, I won't stop you."

In a guttural voice, Suggs replied, "I don't reckon I feel much like walking away."

Darby ran the tip of his tongue over his lips. He growled, "What the blazes you think you're doing, cowboy?"

"I planned on killing you, but I figure jail would be worse. I'm turning you over to the sheriff as soon as I get the name of the last man."

The batwing door swung open right in my face. Suggs grabbed for his sixgun, but Darby shoved him into the jasper leaving the saloon. Both Suggs and the other unlucky soul slammed into me, knocking me backward and sending my sixgun spinning off the boardwalk and into the mud.

Suggs was waving his sixgun over his head while still tangled with the surprised cowpoke. I leaped for the brawny man's wrist, seizing it in both hands. I slammed his hand against the wall of the saloon in an effort to batter the sixgun from his hand.

He stepped forward and swung his left at me, but stumbled on the poor cowpoke squirming under our feet, causing his fist to graze my jaw. Still, I heard bells and saw stars. Right then I knew this fight would be like trying to hogtie a wildcat with a piece of string.

I slammed his gun hand against the wall again, knocking the revolver free and sending it skittering down the boardwalk. I turned to him just as he threw another left. I ducked. His fist slammed into the wall.

Suggs jerked his hand back and cursed.

I stepped forward and did my best to smash his flat nose even flatter. He stumbled back and bounced off a post supporting the porch. As he lunged forward, he shot a straight right that caught me coming in. I stopped in my tracks, and he hooked a left into my stomach. I grunted in pain. He was three inches taller and at least fifty pounds heavier than me.

Putting all my body into it, I dug a left hook into his kidney. He winced, so I put a right hook in the kidney on the other side. That must have just aggravated him, for he hurled a right into my left cheekbone. I felt the bone bend.

He pounded my chest with a left. I retaliated with a crossing right that bounced off his forehead. He countered with a roundhouse right that would have taken my head off if I hadn't ducked.

I caught my breath and sent a sizzling left at his face. My fist caught him on his eyebrow and split the skin. Blood gushed.

With a roar of pain and anger, he lowered his head and charged, catching me in the belly and sending us both through the glass window, crashing into several of those gathered behind the window watching the fight. We were a tangle of arms and legs.

I stumbled to my feet and looked around for my adversary. I found him when he smashed a chair on my back, sending me sprawling to the floor under a table.

He came after me, holding a table leg over his head like a club. I scooted farther under the table and kicked it at him, sending him stumbling backward.

I leaped to my feet and tore a leg from the table I had kicked over. I tasted blood, my own, from the split below my eye.

Suggs climbed to his feet, leering at me all the while. Blood dripped down his cheek and fell on his chest. Of the two of us, I figured he was bleeding more.

He waved the club over his head. "I'm going to beat your head into the mud, cowboy."

We circled each other warily. He was larger than me, but I figured I was quicker. I sure hoped I was.

With a roar of anger, he leaped forward, swinging the leg at my head. I ducked, then slammed my club into the back of his shoulder.

He spun back around. Clenching his rotting teeth, he emitted a guttural roar like an animal and stomped toward me, swinging the club back and forth.

I stepped back, parrying the blows, looking for an opening, waiting for him to tire. His black eyes glittered with obsession. He had only one passion in his brain, to crush my skull. By the time he'd backed me halfway across the saloon, I figured he wasn't going to tire.

Abruptly, I ducked under his swing and raced past him. I headed for the stairs leading up to the mezzanine, hoping they might give me the advantage. I stopped at the bottom of the staircase.

So obsessed was Suggs with swinging his club that he swung twice more after I dodged around him. Finally, he lumbered around and stared at me. Throwing out his arms like a gorilla, he rushed me, waving the table leg.

The stairs did not give me the advantage I wanted. Like a machine he took one step with each swing, ignoring the glancing blows I got in on him. Halfway up, I turned and sprinted to the top, where I grabbed tables, chairs, whatever I could put my hands on, and threw them down at the lumbering giant as he stalked upward.

By now, I was desperate. I didn't have a glimmer of an idea what to do.

At the top of the stairs, Suggs took another swing. I ducked and slammed my club into his doubled fists. He screamed, and his club went flying. He glared at me, his bloody face a mask of rage, blind, raw rage that could be sated only with blood—unfortunately, my blood. If he got to me, I knew he would rip my arms and legs off just like I was a grasshopper.

He clenched his fists and tensed his muscles and from deep in his soul came a wrenching cry. He lowered his head and charged. I jumped aside and slammed the table leg across his back. The leg broke, one end spinning across the mezzanine.

Still with his back to me, Suggs paused and looked around, searching for me. Later, all I could ever figure was that the hate pouring from him so numbed his brain that for a few seconds, he didn't realize I wasn't in front of him.

Behind me, the stairway was jammed with curious spectators, eliminating that as a possible exit.

Before I had time to consider other possibilities, Suggs turned and growled at me like a wild animal. He bared his teeth. "Here it comes," I muttered, at the same time taking a step aside in an effort to find enough room to dodge his next charge.

With a growl of rage, he lunged forward, his brawny shoulders lowered, his head down. He came at me like a locomotive, one I knew I couldn't stop.

All I could do was evade him this time and worry about next time when next time got here.

At the last second, I jumped aside. Before I could turn around, I heard a loud crash and a terrified scream. I spun. The smashed railing dangled over the edge of the mezzanine, and Suggs was nowhere to be seen.

Chapter Fourteen

Standing between the shattered rails on the edge of the mezzanine, I peered down at Suggs' inert form. His arms and legs were spread in a sprawl, but his head was cocked at an unnatural angle.

I touched my fingers to the side of my face, which was tender and swollen. I watched as the bartender knelt beside the motionless man. He slipped his hand under Suggs' chest. He looked up and shook his head. "Dead."

At that moment, Cyrus rushed through the batwing door. He looked around until he spotted me on the mezzanine. He waved frantically. "Jed! Jed! Darby's getting on the steamboat. Hurry!"

I shoved through the crowd and stumbled down the stairs. At the bottom, the bartender grabbed my arm. "Hey, pal. You gotta stay here 'til the sheriff comes."

I jerked my arm away. "You tell him what happened."

Cyrus had my dun beside the boardwalk. I leaped in the saddle, and he handed me my Colt. "I cleaned it best I could."

Slamming the revolver in my holster, I spurred the dun toward the docks.

By the time we reached the dock, the *Captain Howard* was in mid-stream, smoke pouring from its stacks as it churned upriver at three miles an hour.

We sat on our ponies at the edge of the dock, staring after the slowly shrinking steamboat. To my surprise, Cyrus uttered a curse, then said, "Ain't that our luck. Five minutes, and we'd have had him."

I shot him a blistering look. "Hey, boy. You watch your mouth. You're too young to cuss. I'll whop you good next time."

His eyes widened in surprise, then he dropped his gaze to the wooden dock at our feet.

"You hear me?" I barked.

He nodded slowly. "Yes, sir."

That's when I should have realized I would probably keep him, but I didn't. I still planned on dropping him off with Arch and Mary Catherine.

Mary Catherine. Just the thought of her name made me warm inside. To my surprise, I found myself wishing that I had made something of myself, instead of traipsing all around the country looking for those jaspers. Yet I knew I would never have done any different. I reckoned fate just never intended hombres like me such a blessing as a fine woman like her. As an afterthought, I wondered if Arch ever got over whatever was bothering him that last day.

"What now, Jed?"

"Huh?" Jerked from my maudlin reverie, I stared dumbly at Cyrus.

"I said, what do we do now?" He pointed to the steamboat.

"Why, we follow along, naturally. What else? Let's go."

I reined around and stared down at the muzzle of a sixshooter almost in my face. The mustachioed hombre holding it had a star pinned to his chest. He was slender and straight like a cedar post, but I recognized the determination in his eyes. Casually, as if we were old friends, he said, "Reckon I don't need to ask if you was that feller in the fight down at the Red Dog Saloon. That cut on your face and the shiner you're sporting answers the question for me." He motioned me toward the sheriff's office. "I need to have a talk with you, friend. Over there."

I glanced fretfully at the *Captain Howard* as it steamed out of sight around a bend in the river. I turned back to the sheriff. "Can't it wait? I got mighty important business when that boat pulls in upriver."

The sound of a cocking hammer was answer enough, but the sheriff made sure I understood. "You ain't going nowhere until we have us a coroner's inquest. Now git." He noticed Cyrus for the first time. "That your boy?"

"We been riding together," I replied, a testy edge on my words. I resisted the urge to rip the sixshooter from his hand and kick his rear end across the street. Contrary to what some folk might say, I always tried to follow the law.

"You got anyplace to stay, boy?"

"No, sir." Cyrus shook his head.

He looked back to me. "Got any money, cowboy?"

"Not a cent."

Stroking his sandy mustache, the sheriff pondered the situation a moment. "Look, boy," he said to Cyrus. "Stable your horses down at the livery. Tell the liveryman to bill the sheriff's office. I got to put your friend here in the calaboose, but you're welcome to take your meals with him, if you got a mind to."

All of a sudden, the sheriff wasn't the trashy vermin I was figuring. He seemed like a decent sort of man. Maybe sort of set in his ways, but decent. I dismounted, handed Cyrus the reins, removed my gunbelt, and looped it over the saddle horn. "Do what the sheriff says, Cyrus. Then come on over to the jail."

By the time Cyrus had taken care of the animals and come in to stand next to the wall, I had explained all that had taken place to the sheriff, who stared down at his desk and shook his head slowly. "I reckon I'd sure like to help, Mister Walker, but up until a few months back, we had a regular war here in Madison between different families with different political ideas. We came in and enforced the law—tight, but fair. I don't rightly see how I can turn you loose, then go out and arrest one of them should they break the law."

As much as I hated to admit it, I understood exactly what he meant. With a shrug, I stepped into the cell and closed the door after me. "How long before the inquiry?"

Rising from his desk, he locked the cell door. He brushed his drooping mustache from the side of his lips. "Tomorrow. Next day at the latest. Beaumont borrowed our magistrate for a trial."

Two days? I tried to rearrange my strategy. "Sheriff, what are the first couple stops the *Captain Howard* makes on its upriver run?"

He thought a moment. "Reckon the first is Salem's Landing. Then another twelve, fifteen miles up, it pulls in for a load of firewood."

"You think I might be out of here in time to catch it when it pulls in to load up the wood?"

With a grimace, he shrugged. "Close. But, Mister Walker, that steamboat ain't going nowhere. It's a'coming right back down here."

With a wry chuckle, I replied, "Reckon so, but the jasper I'm after won't."

The sheriff glanced at Cyrus. "Come with me over to the café, boy. You can bring you and Mister Walker some noon dinner."

I paced the cell, stopping at each turn to stare out the barred window in the direction the *Captain Howard* had taken. I was so close. I fought against the impatience urging me to break out. I'd always tried to go by the law, as little as there might be in the West. The law was the only way this great country could grow, and though I figured I'd never contribute much at all to it, I could at least follow the laws it set down.

That feeling was sorely put to the test when Cyrus returned with two cloth-covered platters, from which rose tendrils of steam. He wore a frown on his face. He slid my platter under the bars and plopped down cross-legged on the floor next to the cell door. He leaned forward, and in an urgent whisper, said, "Jed, listen! When I was waiting for the lady to dish up our dinner, I heard some fancy-dressed man tell the sheriff the magistrate wouldn't be back for another week. Another trial or something."

I could only stare at Cyrus as his words soaked into my stunned brain. "A week?"

He nodded, his face glum.

I plopped back on the bunk. Woodenly, I set the plate of grub at my side on the mattress.

Cyrus removed the cloth from his plate, revealing a heaping portion of fried chicken, three hot biscuits, and enough thick cream gravy to cover it all. Cyrus poked in a mouthful, and while he was chewing, managed to mumble, "What now?"

What now? I had no idea. My head was emptier than a gutted steer. "I got to ponder the matter," I muttered, absently removing the cloth from my plate and staring down at the food for which I now had no taste.

I cursed myself for letting the sheriff stick my worthless carcass in jail. "I should have ridden out," I muttered, looking out through the barred window.

"What did you say, Jeb?" Cyrus' words were garbled by the ball of grub he had in his mouth. He was putting a mighty big hurt on that plateful of vittles.

With a grunt, I sat back on the bunk. "I'm not certain. All I know is if I give Darby a week, he'll get himself so lost I'll never find him again."

Cyrus paused in his chomping and frowned at me. He pointed to the wall. "There's the keys, Jed. You want me to let you out?"

The keys! Why hadn't I noticed the keys on the peg? I studied the matter. I could slip out, settle my problems with Darby, and then come back. Yeah. That would solve everything.

I grinned at Cyrus, but before I could say yes, the sheriff came back in, strode across the floor to the keys, jammed them in his hip pocket, and gave me a sheepish grin. "Forgot about these things." He eyed Cyrus, then grinned at me. "No sense in placing too much temptation in a body's way."

With a long sigh, I replied, "Reckon not, Sheriff." I didn't want to let on I knew about the delay. "But, I don't plan on going nowhere. I can afford a day or two." I waited for his reply.

He coughed and glanced out the door. He then took a deep breath and stepped closer to the cell, looking me in the eye. "Mister Walker, I got to be honest with you. It won't be no day or two. The mayor just told me our magistrate is held over in Beaumont for another week, maybe two." He shook his head, and I truly believe he felt bad for me. "I can see how important all that is to you. I'm truly sorry." He looked at me for another moment, nodded, then turned back to the door. Over his shoulder, he spoke to Cyrus. "Take them plates and utensils back to the café when you all finish, boy."

"Yes, sir," Cyrus replied in a respectful voice, at the same time winking at me.

After the sheriff left, Cyrus shook his head. "I shoulda thought about the keys sooner."

I shook my head. "Wasn't your fault, son." With a groan, I picked up a chicken leg. Since I was going to be in here a spell, I figured I might as well eat.

Cyrus looked on thoughtfully while I ate. From the way he had eaten, I knew the grub must be tasty, but to me it had the flavor of wood shavings.

He reached for my plate when I was finished. "Anything else, Jed?"

I shook my head.

"I'll be back directly, Jed," he said, closing the door behind him.

When he returned, he told me he had heard that almost five hundred Mexican steers had bedded down east of town. They were being pushed to New Orleans. The next morning, the wranglers planned to swim them across the Sabine.

I listened without any enthusiasm. "Just you watch yourself in the morning, boy. Stay off the street. Anything spooks those beeves, not even a tornado can stop them."

A frown wrinkled his forehead. A few moments later, an odd grin played over his lips. He jumped up. "I'll be back after a while, Jed."

Two or three times during the afternoon, he popped in, asked how I was, gave me a puzzling grin, then left.

During the afternoon, I heard a voice geehawing a team out back, and when I looked out, I spotted Cyrus parking a wagon a few feet from the back of the jail. Fifteen minutes later, he brought a second team around, parking the wagon beside the first.

"Helping the liveryman," he said, when I asked what he was up to. "For stabling our horses. He said I could sleep there tonight."

About sundown, he brought supper. He seemed edgy, nervous, but claimed he was just fine when I questioned him. After a couple games of checkers, he rose, stretched, and declared he was sleepy.

I lay in my bunk, my hands behind my head, staring at the ceiling above for what seemed like hours. Well, I guessed I would be starting all over again in my search for the last two men. I had done it several times, so I figured I could do it again.

The sheriff snored on his bunk against the far wall.

Suddenly, gunshots rang out east of town, followed by the frightened bellows of five hundred head of Mexican steers. The sheriff bolted from the jail. The town erupted in shouts and gunfire. Horses raced back and forth.

A few moments later, a shadow appeared at the window and deftly wound a rope around two of the bars. "Jed! Your horse is tied to the tree at the back corner of the jail. The road north of town is behind the Red Dog Saloon."

I squinted into the darkness. Cyrus! Before I could say a word, he spurred his horse around in front of the two teams he had parked earlier, grabbed the lead ropes he had tied to them, and with a shout, galvanized the eight horses into a gallop.

The wagons leaped forward, the ropes snapped taut, and with a shriek of splitting wood, the window ripped from the wall. Grabbing my hat, I jumped from the window and sprinted for my pony.

As I swung into the saddle, I saw Cyrus drop the ropes and cut east. The horses and wagons disappeared into the darkness.

Leaning low over the dun, I raced up the dark alley, trying to pick out the Red Dog Saloon from the back. Ahead, in the pale light cast by the open door of the Red Dog, I spotted Cyrus astride his pony.

Some cowpoke had stopped him and was holding onto the reins. The hombre seemed mighty excited and kept pointing in the direction the herd had bedded.

I didn't know what he was saying, but at the moment, I didn't care, so I did what any common-sense cowpoke would do. I ran over him.

Chapter Fifteen

I didn't hit him square on, but it wasn't my fault. When the hombre saw my intention, he threw himself backward. By the time he scrambled to his feet, we had vanished into the darkness.

The stars provided our only light, a dim, bluish glow that permitted us to discern the road before us but offered no other illumination. The tall pines and ancient oaks on either side formed a black wall a hundred feet high.

We rode for a couple hours. "Pull up," I called out, tightening the reins. "We're a good piece from town. I don't reckon the sheriff will go to all the trouble to follow me just because of an inquest. But, we best take no chances. We'll pull off into the forest a piece and make a cold camp."

Pulling into the forest a short piece was easier said

than done. The starlight could not penetrate the canopy of leaves above. We dismounted and led our ponies. In places, the forest was blacker than a black cat's overcoat, forcing us to feel our way from trunk to trunk.

After about ten minutes, I halted. "This should be far enough."

We tethered our horses and rolled out our soogans. I planned on questioning Cyrus about how he managed to pull off my escape, but within seconds after his head hit the blankets, he was asleep, a well-deserved sleep after all the little man had carried out.

I lay in the darkness, listening to the sounds of the forest around us. My plans were no more elaborate than reaching Salem's Landing by sundown the next day, and if I could find no trace of Darby, try to reach the *Captain Howard* while it was loading wood.

Morning drifted through the forest like a fog, slowly erasing the shadows across the forest floor. We built a small fire and put together a hot breakfast.

Fifteen minutes later, we rode out. "I reckon we're about twenty miles or so from Salem's Landing," I said, studying the road we had traveled in the opposite direction weeks earlier. We passed a peddler of pots and pans and a couple hours later, a wagonload of fresh-cut planks.

Mid-morning, a plaintive cry drifted through the dark woods around us. Cyrus and I looked at each other. As one, we reined up our ponies.

Several seconds of absolute silence passed. Just as we started to ride on, the almost inaudible cry came again. Cyrus looked at me, his wide eyes clearly revealing the apprehension the cries sent through him like electrical charges. He whispered, "Indians?"

I shucked my sixgun. "I don't know."

The cry came again.

"What's he saying?"

"I can't make it out."

"Someone might be bad hurt."

"Maybe," I replied, studying the forest from where the cry had come. "Maybe not."

In a small, strangled voice, Cyrus asked, "We going to see what it is?"

I wasn't crazy enough to try to hug a grizzly, but what if this wasn't a grizzly? What if it was some jasper needing help?

Impatiently, Cyrus asked again, "Are we? Huh? Are we going to see what it is?"

I tugged my Stetson down tight on my head. "I am. You're staying right here. If it's a trap, get to Salem's Landing. Let them know."

"But, Jed. I want to—"

I snapped at him. "No argument, Cyrus. No argument at all, you hear? If it is a trap, you get your little carcass to Salem's Landing as fast as you can. Don't stop for nothing."

With a click of my tongue, I urged my dun into the forest. The winter sleet and rain had softened the needles and leaves on the forest floor, muffling my passage through the giant pines and century-old oaks.

The cry came again, back northeast, this time more distinct. It was a cry for help.

I scanned the shadowy forest about me, searching for any indication of bushwhackers. By now, I could hear the sound of rushing water. The river was nearby, and that meant that whoever or whatever was crying out had to be directly in front of me.

Then I spotted a shadow straight ahead, a shadow unlike any cast by the trees. I reined up and cocked my sixgun. For several seconds, I stood still, waiting for the shadow to move.

It remained motionless.

With a gentle nudge of my knees, I put the dun into a slow walk. Suddenly, his ears perked forward and he whinnied.

The shadow ahead of me moved and whinnied. A horse. Someone's horse. At that second, another cry for help echoed through the forest, this time stronger and more urgent.

Every muscle tensed as I continued forward, my finger tight on the trigger, ready to fire, slam my spurs into my pony, and duck all at the same time.

Ahead, the forest floor dropped away into a shallow depression. The depression led to a deep gully.

The cry came again, this time from the gully.

My dun whinnied, and the second horse replied. The shadows surrounding the trunks of the huge trees took on an ominous presence. I reined up when I got a good look at the horse—an Indian pony, ground reined at the edge of the gully with only a Saltillo blanket for a saddle and a larks-head knot around the pony's lower jaw that served as a bridle.

I pulled up beside the pony and glanced down in the gully. I grimaced. Fifteen feet below lay a young Indian boy on his back, one leg twisted at an unnatural angle.

When he saw me, his eyes grew wide. Even at that distance, I saw the fear in them. Quickly, I holstered my sixgun and held up one hand. "No hurt. No hurt."

He didn't understand me, for he moaned and tried desperately to scoot away on his back. I held up my first two fingers up in the sign of friendship I'd picked up from the Santee Sioux up in Nebraska a few years earlier.

He jerked his head around, searching for an escape. I muttered under my breath. If the boy kept squirming around, he'd sure as thunder punch one end of those broken bones through his skin. As a last resort, I tried the sign for "friend" that I'd learned from one of the southern tribes of Indians. I linked my index fingers in front of my chest, my elbows extended.

He stopped squirming. A look of disbelief flickered across his face. I nodded and raised my linked fingers to my face. I then pointed at him and at me, then linked the fingers again.

With a terse nod, he let me know he understood. He might have understood, but he didn't really believe me, for when I dismounted, his eyes grew wide. But then when I removed the canteen from the saddle horn, he began to relax.

Climbing down into the gully, I knelt at his side and offered the canteen. He grabbed it, then paused. Despite his thirst, he took only two swallows, then handed it back to me. I shook my head and motioned for him to drink. He took two more swallows and watched stoically as I gently touched his leg. He winced, but made not a sound.

Rising, I touched my chest, pointed back to the road, and held my right hand in front of me, index finger extended and pointing upward in the sign for "son." My son. I tried to make him understand I was going for Cyrus.

He nodded. I motioned to the canteen and his lips. He understood, turning it up for another drink.

Ten minutes later, Cyrus and I were attending the young boy, who I guessed was probably about the same age as Cyrus. While I split the boy's trousers with my knife, Cyrus gathered sticks for splints and unwound a few feet of his leather reata lasso to bind them.

The youth watched silently. The break was a few inches below the knee. I gently touched the area. He flinched, tears coming to his eyes, but he remained silent.

"Is it going to hurt, Jed?"

I shook my head at Cyrus. "Afraid so, boy."

Cyrus gave the Indian boy a weak grin and nodded. The boy nodded back.

Sitting back on my heels, I went through the motions of what I was going to do so the young Indian would know what to expect. I didn't know the sign for "pain" or "hurt," so I mimicked striking my shin, then grabbed it, and squeezed my eyes shut.

When I looked at the youth, I could see understanding in his eyes. He nodded.

I gave him a stick to bite on, then pressed him back on the ground. "All right, Cyrus. Kneel behind him and hold his hands. Let him squeeze yours clean off if that helps the hurt."

Cyrus gulped. His own face had paled. "Can—can we really fix his leg, Jed?"

"You bet, boy." I grinned. "During the war, just before those Union boys captured me, I busted my leg. Set it myself. Hooked my foot in the fork of a tree and straightened it right out. This boy here, he's going to be just fine." I grinned at the Indian boy and nodded again.

He forced a wan smile.

The only good I've ever found in pain is that sometimes it knocks you out so the real work can take place. I suppose that's nature's way of getting us healed, for if we remained conscious, we'd probably pitch such a fit from the pain that the job would only get half done.

As soon as I straightened his leg, the young Indian boy fainted. I worked quickly, muttering a silent prayer of thanks that the break was no worse that it had been. Soon, he was splinted and bound up good and proper.

When I finished, I leaned back and breathed a long sigh of relief. Cyrus and me exchanged big grins, and then I remembered Darby. I shook my head. Seemed like everything was on his side.

While the Indian boy slept, Cyrus rode to the river and returned with a string of catfish. We soon had a small fire going with coffee boiling, and we put the catfish on spits to broil.

We spent the night in the gully. Best we could understand, the youth's name was Horse In Water. And with the use of sign, I learned his family was somewhere between here and the Neches River to the west.

Next morning we rode out, due west. Another day or so wasted, but I had to get the Indian boy back to his own folks. I tried to put Darby from my mind, but like a cancer, he remained. The boys rode behind me, and I could hear pieces of their broken conversation.

I suppose the reason I didn't see the war party ahead was because I was feeling so sorry for myself. One moment, we were riding across the forest floor beneath giant pines and the next, we were surrounded by half a dozen glowering Indians, all with Winchesters or Spencers, and all pointed right at us.

Horse In Water cried out and spurred his pony forward, stopping in front of the one who appeared to be their chief. He spoke rapidly, gesturing to us, to his leg, and to his stomach.

As if by magic, their grim visages became impassive. The chief rode up to me, his face inscrutable. In broken English, he said, "My son, he say you help doctor leg." He tapped his fist against his chest. "Me Tall Cougar. You good man. Many thanks."

My mouth was too dry to form any words. All I could do was nod.

Before they rode out, Horse In Water came back to us. He slipped his knife from its scabbard and handed it to Cyrus and linked his index fingers. With a nod, he rode back to the others, and moments later they had disappeared silently into the forest.

Cyrus pulled up to my side. "Isn't this a fine knife?"

"Sure is, boy."

"Why'd he give it to me, Jed?"

"You notice the sign he made afterward?"

"You mean when he hooked his fingers in front of his chest?"

"Yep. That's how he says friendship."

Cyrus didn't answer. He just stared at the knife.

I turned my pony back toward the road. "Let's go, Cyrus. With luck, we might reach Salem's Landing by sundown."

Chapter Sixteen

We reached Salem's Landing just before sundown. From the shipping clerk, we were given good news and bad news. The bad news was that the *Captain Howard* already had pulled out, but the good news was that it had laid over an extra day for emergency maintenance on the paddle wheel. The steamboat had shoved off just that morning.

"Did any passengers get off?"

"Reckon so. Seeing the sights, such as they are," he said, gesturing to the four rough buildings comprising the small village.

"I mean, did any leave?"

"Nope. Reckon not. If they did, I didn't see them."

"How long does it take the boat to reach the wood racks?"

The clerk pursed his thin lips. The flickering lamplight gave his face a sallow look. "Not long, twelve hours, more or less. Normally, they tie up for the night and load during the day, but I reckon they'll be working all night tonight to make up for lost time."

I thanked the old man, and pausing only to buy a couple cans of peaches, we pounded up the trace toward the firewood racks.

We rode hard, pushing our ponies. Sometime before midnight, we spotted lights through the forest.

"Whoa, boy," I whispered to my dun, pulling on the reins. "Let's us take it nice and slow, Cyrus."

We walked our ponies, pulling up at the last bend before the trace reached the landing. A long row of lanterns stretched from the bow of the *Captain Howard*, over the gangplank, and up the shore to the stacked cords of firewood.

Music and laughter came from the boat, a sharp contrast to the sight of the sweating deckhands hauling log after log on their shoulders across the shore, up the gangplank, and back to the boilers.

From where we sat astride our ponies, I knew no one could see us.

I faced a dilemma. What if Darby had some connection with the *Captain Howard*? Last time I'd questioned the captain of the steamboat, he was no help, although he did ask his bosun.

I peered at the individual at the log pile who seemed to be directing the loading. I wondered if he was the same bosun as back in Madison.

Should I take the chance and ask him? Or should I slip aboard and try to find Darby?

Moving quickly, I dismounted and handed Cyrus my reins. While I removed my spurs, I gave him instructions. "I'm going to slip aboard. If I'm not off by the time they leave in the morning, follow along on the road. Their next stop should be Burkeville."

He nodded silently. I looped my gunbelt over the saddlehorn and slipped the sixgun under my belt and buttoned the Mackinaw over it. I looked up at Cyrus. "You be careful, you hear?" I removed my hat and tucked it inside my coat.

He nodded. "You too," he replied in a croaking voice.

Staying in a crouch, I circled the log pile, keeping it between me and the bosun. I moved to the end of one pile and waited for my chance. It came moments later, when bosun glanced toward the boat. I stepped in front of one of the deckhands, hefting a log on my shoulder, and followed after the deckhand in front.

The one behind muttered, "Hey, who are you?"

"New hand," I said.

He chuckled. "You shoulda found yourself a better job."

We carried the logs along the port deck and stacked them near the boilers. On the way back for another load, I faked a stumble near the shadows cast by the ladder leading to the second deck.

The deckhand behind me cursed. "What's wrong with you?"

"Nothing. Turned an ankle. You go on. I'll be right behind."

With a grunt, he headed back to the bow, and I quickly disappeared into the shadows of an adjoining passageway. Removing my hat and straightening it, I sat back in a corner and considered my next move. With luck, no one would pay me any attention. With my hat and Mackinaw, I looked like any other passenger.

And with a little extra luck, I could mingle with them and find Darby.

The *Captain Howard* was neither as large nor as elaborate as the Mississippi steamboats. The main gallery was almost deserted, most revelers having retired to their staterooms. A dozen or so hard-core gamblers persisted in just one more hand of poker.

At the far end of the gallery, a couple sat over the remains of their supper, touching glasses of champagne.

While several of the jaspers at the poker tables were dressed in duds similar to mine, I knew if I remained around too long, I would draw attention.

Casually, I sauntered past the tables, eyeing the players, pausing to watch a hand, then moving on.

No Darby.

Stepping from the gallery, I pulled my Stetson down over my eyes and strolled the deck. A few small clusters of men stood about, smoking their cigars, discussing the latest news of Reconstruction, and wondering about the coming year's price of cotton.

One party stopped me as I passed. "Excuse me, sir."

I froze, expecting to be exposed as a stowaway. I looked around. "Me?"

A neatly dressed gentleman wearing a gray frock coat over a white vest and ruffled shirt stepped forward. "My name's Langdon Beauchamp. You look like a cowman." He gestured to a member of his party. "We were discussing the price of beef. I claim a man makes more driving beef to the railhead in Kansas than by driving them to New Orleans." He paused and took a long drag on his cigar. "What do you think?"

I had no idea of the price of beef in Kansas or New Orleans, but obviously, they had no idea that I had no idea. "Well, sir, I reckon I'd take them to Kansas. Prices are better, and even after a jasper pays off the boys, he'll keep more of his profit."

Beauchamp jabbed his cigar at his friend. "See. What did I tell you, John?" He turned back to me and doffed his hat. "Much obliged, sir. You've just won me twenty dollars. I would consider it an honor if you—"

I interrupted him as I backed away. "Glad to help, sir. Glad to help." I turned and hurried away.

After two or three turns around the upper and lower decks without spotting Darby, I found a secluded closet and huddled down for the night.

* * *

The shuddering vibration resonating through the hull of the *Captain Howard* as the vessel got underway next morning awakened me. Rising, I stretched the cramps from my muscles before stepping out on the deck.

A few early morning strollers were out, but no one paid me any attention. I kept my eyes peeled for the captain and the bosun, the only two who might possibly recognize me.

My stomach growled. I had not put anything down my gullet for the last twenty-four hours, and my belly was shaking hands with my backbone.

I peered into the main gallery. Succulent aromas of ham, eggs, and coffee filled the room. Half a dozen tables were already filled with early risers. A few passengers were serving themselves from the array of silver serving warmers set up on the credenzas draped with white linen cloths.

A couple cowpokes pulled up to the end of the line. I decided to join them.

One nodded to me. "Morning."

I grinned. "Morning."

He shook his head. "I don't know about you, but I ain't used to sleeping on something that keeps rocking all night."

We both laughed as he filled his plate.

I followed right behind him, helping myself to the mounds of eggs and ham.

At the head of the line stood a deckhand. I couldn't

tell what he was doing, but he seemed to be talking to each of the passengers and jotting something on a sheet of paper in his hand as they left the buffet.

Then he spoke to the cowpoke ahead of me. "What room are you in, sir?" I froze, then hastily glanced around the gallery, searching for a way out. I spotted Langdon Beauchamp, the dandy who had stopped me the night before.

"Sir. Sir."

I looked back around. "Huh? Oh, sorry. What can I do for you?"

He indicated the list in his hand. "What room are you in, sir?"

"Sorry, I don't remember, but it's with Mister Beauchamp over there. See? Over there by the door." I waved, hoping Beauchamp would spot me.

He did, and to my relief, returned my wave.

The deckhand nodded and thanked me.

After a filling breakfast, during which I kept watching the passengers for Darby, I headed for the decks again. The morning passed slowly. I was beginning to wonder if maybe Darby had disembarked back at Salem's Landing.

Though the sun shone brightly, the north wind coming off the river carried a chill, and I was grateful each time I went back into the warm gallery. Just before dinner, I opened the door to the gallery and ran face to face with Beauchamp.

He grinned and held up his walking stick in recognition. "Ah, my friend from last night."

"Morning," I replied with a nod, attempting to step around him.

He quickly stepped in my path, still with that amiable smile on his face. "No sense in hurrying. I'd be pleased if you'd take dinner with me." He paused a few seconds and his smile grew broader. "Especially since it appears I paid for your breakfast."

I tried to think fast, but his words caused my brain to turn thicker than gumbo mud. I glanced past him, half expecting to see the captain or the bosun carrying leg chains. But no one paid us any attention. I forced a grin. "Sorry, Mister Beauchamp. I was hungry, and I was broke, and I couldn't afford the captain to throw me over."

He pursed his lips and gestured to the noon buffet with the silver head of his walking cane. "I've been in those circumstances myself, friend. Let me invite you to dinner. The repast is nothing to compare with finer restaurants, but for a vessel such as this, it is quite tasty."

I studied him a moment. I had nothing to lose, and possibly one more solid meal before I was tossed in the brig. "After you, Mister Beauchamp."

"You suppose I might know with whom I'm having the pleasure of dining?"

With a sheepish grin, I stuck out my hand. "Jed Walker, formerly of Missouri, recently of most of the United States."

Beauchamp might not have been too impressed with the dinner of beef stew, but I was. And the coffee was some of the best I had tasted. Beauchamp was a like-able jasper, a Georgian plantation owner by birth, cur-rently a gambler by trade, and from his cool demeanor and the obvious dexterity of his slender fingers, quite accomplished at the trade.

After he heard my story, he removed a cigar from a silver case, offered me one, and touched a match to both. He leaned back in his chair. "Quite a formidable task you've held yourself too for all these years."

With a shrug, I replied, "There wasn't much of a choice. My ma always taught me an eye for an eye."

He smiled at me. "Religious lady."

I sipped my coffee. "Yes."

"After what those Yankees did to my family during the war, religion became of secondary concern to me, Mister Walker. I do remember, however, a verse somewhere in the Bible. I think it was Mark, chapter nine, verse forty-seven. 'If thine eye offend thee, pluck it out.' "

I didn't remember ever hearing that verse, but I fig-ured anyone who could quote book, chapter, and verse must know what he was talking about.

"Maybe so, but sometimes that eye can prove itself to be mighty stubborn."

He laughed. "I suppose it can."

I polished off my coffee. As I rose to leave, Beau-champ looked up at me. "This Darby. How was he dressed when he came aboard?"

"Gray Stetson, leather vest, two sixguns, high on

his waist. He stands about six feet or so, a couple inches taller than me."

He rose and looked me in the eye. "If I spot him, I'll let you know."

I offered him my hand. "Thanks . . . Langdon."

"You're quite welcome, Jed."

There was no time for Beauchamp to look for Darby, for when I opened the door to step on deck, I stared Darby in the face.

For a moment, we gaped at each other. Before he could move, I grabbed his vest and yanked him inside the gallery. He tried to catch his balance as he stumbled over a table and chairs. I leaped after him, jumping on his back and straddling him when he fell to the floor.

Finally, after twelve long years.

Chapter Seventeen

Darby squirmed onto his back and threw a straight right that hit me between the eyes. I rocked back, then jerked forward, pounding my fists into his face, vaguely aware of the shouting around us.

Suddenly, rough hands jerked me up and pinned my arms behind my back.

Darby jumped to his feet. Blood poured from his nose. He stepped forward and threw a wild right at my jaw, but I ducked and whoever was holding me grunted and dropped my arms. I waded into Darby, swinging my arms like pile drivers, pounding his belly.

Hands seized me again. This time, Darby was jerked away from me.

"What the sam hill is going on here?" The captain glared at us like Moses down from the mountain.

160

Straining against the two burly deckhands holding him, Darby blurted out, "This jasper jumped me for no blasted reason. I want him in jail. I insist you put him in the brig."

I tried to break loose, but my arms were pinned securely. Desperately, I cried out, "This man shot and killed my brother twelve years ago in Missouri. I've been after him since."

"He's lying, Captain. I ain't never been to Missouri."

Forcing myself to calm down, I said, "Look, Captain. All I'm asking is that you keep both of us under lock and key and turn us over to the sheriff down in Madison." I didn't really know what good I could gain from that, but at least it would prevent Darby's escape.

The captain frowned as he considered my request. "I seem to remember you from somewhere."

"Yes. A few weeks ago down in Madison, I came aboard and talked to you about another man. You called the bosun in."

He nodded. "Yes, now I remember." His frown deepened. "But I don't remember seeing you on this voyage."

"I came aboard when you were loading firewood last night."

"Stowaway?" His face darkened.

"No. Not exactly."

Darby saw his chance. "I told you, Captain. This jasper is nothing but trouble. I say throw him in the brig and turn him over to the sheriff when you get back to Madison."

I had a feeling my credibility with the captain had sunk to a new low.

And then along came Langdon Beauchamp. In his smooth, well-modulated voice, he said, "If I may, Captain. I can vouch for Mister Walker here. I have known his family for years, a fine Missouri family with Southern leanings, leanings that the Yankees used as an excuse to destroy their fine old homestead. I can assure you that Mister Walker speaks the truth."

Darby growled. "Don't listen to him, Captain. He ain't nothing but a riverboat gambler."

Beauchamp raised his cane to make a point. "A gambler, yes, sir, but a Southern gambler from the bosom of Mother Georgia, Atlanta to be precise, just as the captain here."

All that kept Darby's chin from hitting the floor was the toe of his boots. He glared at me, and I gave him a smug grin in return.

The captain nodded to the deckhands. "All right, boys. Lock them two up—in different staterooms."

I couldn't complain about the accommodations. The room was small but snug. I entertained myself with a deck of cards that afternoon until a porter brought my supper. After supper, Langdon Beauchamp showed up with a deck of cards, a handful of cigars, and a bottle of premium brandy.

All that I needed to make my world complete was

to see Darby in jail and to be in possession of the last hombre's name.

That night, the banjo and fiddle music drifted up from the gallery. I thought of Cyrus, and Mary Catherine, and Arch. I couldn't help wondering if Red still called on her. And I also hoped that Arch had gotten over whatever had been eating at him.

We tied up at Burkeville for the night.

Thirty minutes after we sailed next morning, a porter brought breakfast, accompanied by a deckhand with a revolver under his belt. The porter informed me that our progress would be slow today because of the excessive number of logs in the river.

I couldn't help wondering about Darby. I had no hard proof of the murder. My word against his. And that wasn't sufficient.

Maybe I should just kill him, I thought.

Beauchamp visited me later that morning, and during a game of stud poker, we discussed the strategies by which I could prove Darby guilty. Beauchamp shook his head as he dealt me a card. "Too bad the one you called Abner died. He could sustain your contention."

"Or," I replied, "if I could find the fifth man."

Beauchamp smiled grimly. "A thousand to one odds, my friend."

He dealt me a deuce instead of the trey I needed for a small straight. I popped the card on the table. "Then maybe I should shoot him."

With a chuckle, Beauchamp jotted figures on a small pad and gathered the cards for another shuffle. "Then the law would have you. By the way, that's fifty-three dollars you owe me."

With a resigned sigh, I shook my head. He was grinning at me, and I started laughing at my situation. "Don't look like I have any place to go except straight ahead."

"Sometimes that's the best plan, Jed. Besides, not a soul lives who can predict the caprices of fate."

I frowned at his choice of words. With a faint smile, he explained. "Whims, the fickleness of fate."

There was something in what he said, for a moment later, the door swung open and the Captain looked at me. "I'm sorry, Mister Walker, but Darby has escaped. Sometime since breakfast this morning. One of our skiffs is missing. I figured he rowed ashore."

My dreams exploded. I jumped to my feet and rushed to the door. "I've got to get him."

The captain and a deckhand tried to grab me, but I bowled them aside and sprinted along the upper deck to the stern, where I clambered down the ladder to the main deck. I looked around. We were in the middle of the river, which was two hundred yards wide at this point.

Behind me, on the second deck, the captain shouted. I took a couple steps back, then sprinted across the deck, launching myself out over the muddy brown water as far as I could to avoid the suction of the huge paddlewheel propelling the *Captain Howard.*

I gasped in shock when I hit the icy water and sliced beneath the surface. Moments later, I came up swimming, heading for the west shore of the river. By now, the steamboat had passed, and I could see Beauchamp, the captain, and his deckhand on the second deck. They leaned against the railing, watching me.

Beauchamp lifted his arm and pounded his fist against the air.

The swift current swept me downriver. I kept my eyes on the distant shore as I moved past it. I began to feel a chill. I swam harder, trying build body heat against the cold. I clenched my teeth to stop the chattering.

My strength ebbed, but I fought against the savage waters trying to suck me under. In my brain, I created the image of Darby on the shore and fixed my eyes on him. The back of my right leg started cramping. I tried to ignore it, but it grew tighter, more painful, like someone had grabbed the muscle and was attempting to rip it out.

But the shore was drawing closer. I knew I would reach it. I would reach it or die trying. I glimpsed the *Captain Howard*, now disappearing around a bend.

My breathing grew ragged. My arms felt like lead. My legs weighed a thousand pounds. I couldn't stop; my muscles would cramp into painful knots, and there would be no chance of resuming swimming.

Suddenly, Cyrus appeared on the shore, swinging his reata over his head. He waded his pony into the water and tossed me a loop. I grabbed it and stood up. To my surprise, the water came only to my shoulders.

I had made it.

Once ashore, the first question I put to Cyrus was if he had spotted Darby in a skiff earlier that morning.

He grinned at me. "Yes, sir. When I saw the rowboat, I hid and watched him come ashore and head north up the road. He probably ain't more than an hour ahead."

Despite the chills racking my body, I grinned. "That would be Sabinetown."

Cyrus made a roaring fire while I shed my wet duds and slipped into the dry ones I carried in my soogan. I'd left my Mackinaw aboard the *Captain Howard*, so I wrapped myself in my blankets. Cyrus put coffee in the coals and a split rabbit on to broil.

"I followed the boat along the shore when I could," he told me while we sipped coffee and waited for the rabbit. "I was sure surprised when I saw Darby get off."

"I bet you were, but I tell you, Cyrus, you've done right good. Run into any trouble?"

"Nope. When I spotted someone, I ducked off the road or hid in the undergrowth." He laughed. "Sometimes that wasn't any too easy with two horses." He grew serious. "But, you know, sometimes, Jed, I had the feeling I was being watched. Like somebody was spying on me. Ever since you went aboard at the wood yard."

I glanced around the forest, puzzled. I shrugged. "Just your imagination."

He frowned at me, but remained silent.

After we put ourselves around the rabbit and drained the coffee, we pushed out.

Darby's sign was easy to follow on the trace, for the winter rains and sleet had softened the red soil so that tracks cut deep and sharp into it.

As we rode, my mind kept leaping beyond my future confrontation with Darby and the fifth man, leaping ahead to life afterward. I glanced at Cyrus. He was a fine boy. He'd fit it with the Hopkins clan back at the Bar H like one of a matched pair.

Once or twice during the day, I heard a branch snap deep in the forest. I chalked it up to deer or bears.

At dark, we pulled off the road, not wanting to take a chance of passing Darby during the night and perhaps spooking him into changing his plans, which at the present seemed to be reaching Sabinetown.

As far as I knew, Sabinetown was the closet village where Darby could buy a horse and either continue the purpose of his trip upriver or disappear into the sprawling forests that carpeted East Texas.

Next morning, we took up Darby's trail again. At noon, we pulled up around a bend from Sabinetown. Darby's trail led into town. From our vantage point, the pines prevented anyone in town from seeing us, while at the same time providing us a fairly clear picture of the small village. It consisted of two saloons and a general store facing the rude dock along the river's edge.

I pulled my Henry from its boot and laid it across the saddle as we rode in. I scanned the small village, trying to take in every sight.

The shipping clerk at the dock said the *Captain Howard* had put in that morning and shoved off a couple hours later. I described Darby, but the clerk had not seen him.

Back outside, I looked up at Cyrus. "You stay here with the horses. I'll take a look over there," I said, indicating the three log buildings with the muzzle of my Henry.

Cyrus nodded, saying nothing.

At that moment, two riders rode into town from the north road. I gaped when I saw them. Arch and Mary Catherine Hopkins.

Arch waved, and they rode over to us, grinning like the proverbial possum. "Jed! Lord, I didn't think we'd ever find you." He shook my hand, and I just stared dumbly at him.

Then Mary Catherine shook my hand. "We got worried, so we decided to run you down."

I was flabbergasted. Finally, I found enough of my voice to croak out, "H-howdy." I pointed to Cyrus and introduced him.

Arch laughed, but it still wasn't the old laugh, not like at first. It was still sort of nervous. He seemed like he was holding something back. "We come out to help, Jed. If you'll let us." He exchanged looks with

Mary Catherine. She nodded. He cleared his throat. "But first, there's something you need to know."

By now, I had gathered my thoughts. "Not now, Arch. Sorry. I got other business. You two stay here with Cyrus. I got me some business yonder," I said, indicating the three buildings across the street.

Mary Catherine started to protest, but seemed to decide against it.

Only two jaspers were in the first saloon, a dingy, damp room lit by a flickering oil lantern that left a layer of black soot over everything.

I went next door to the general store, a sturdy building constructed of rough-sawn planks. The owner appeared nervous. His gaze flicked over my shoulder to a closed door in the east wall of the building as I described Darby.

He shook his head. "No, sir. Ain't seen nobody like that."

Disappointed, I looked around the room. A soft noise, like the scrape of a boot on wood, came from behind the closed door. I pointed at it with the muzzle of the Henry. "What's in there?"

"Just—just my storeroom. That's all."

I nodded, but it didn't take a genius to see that something had spooked the proprietor. I deliberately kept my eyes from the door. "Thanks, partner," I said in a loud voice. "I'll check next door."

He nodded jerkily, a look of relief on his face.

I opened the door, then slammed it hard, at the same

time dropping down behind a barrel of pickles that hid me from anyone coming out of the storeroom.

The little storekeeper's eyes bulged. I touched my finger to my lips, then pointed to the Henry.

He gulped. His eyes grew wider.

Moments later, the storeroom door squeaked open. The hard thump of boot heels echoed across the room. I heard Darby's guttural voice. "He gone?"

I rose quickly and cocked the Henry. "Not yet, Darby. Don't move."

Chapter Eighteen

Darby froze, his sixgun in hand.

The little man behind the counter gaped.

I eased forward. "All right, Darby. Drop that hog-leg."

Slowly, he lifted his arm out to his side, at the same time easing his fingers from around the butt. Then, he dropped it, at the same time falling to one knee and slapping leather for his other sixgun.

I squeezed off two quick shots, blowing the top off a barrel of flour and shattering a jar of pickled eggs on the counter. The boom of the Henry was deafening.

He popped up and fired off two slugs at me that whizzed over my head and shattered the window behind me. I fired twice more, then ducked behind the barrel, punching more cartridges down the magazine.

"Give it up, Darby. I don't want to kill you." I scooted a few feet to one side, staying behind a counter.

He snarled. "You got it wrong, cowboy. You're the one they'll carry out of here." He fired twice more. Chunks of wood exploded from the barrel behind which I had been hiding.

I jumped up and fired three times. Two missed him, but the third caught his handgun, knocking it from his hand.

He cursed and leaped for it.

I placed two more slugs in front of him. "The next two punch holes in your back, Darby." He jerked to a halt, his chest heaving. His shoulders sagged. "Now turn around."

A smoky haze filled the room, and the acrid stench of gunpowder stung my nostrils.

He stopped beside the barrel of flour and turned to glare at me.

I eased around a counter laden with denim shirts and jeans. I spotted movement in my peripheral vision to my left. For a brief second, I cut my eyes toward the movement and spotted the storeowner sticking his head above the countertop.

I jerked my head back around in time to see a billowing cloud of flour in my face. I fired blindly.

In the next second, a large body slammed into me, knocking me backwards and sending the Henry rifle flying from my hands.

"It's my turn now, cowboy," Darby growled, straddling me and slamming heavy blows to my head. I fended off his punches as best I could while trying to land some of my own. I blinked against the blinding flour and felt the dampness of blood mingling with the soft whiteness.

Through a haze, I saw Darby lean forward on his knees. I jerked my own knees up sharply, catching him in the rear and sending him toppling over my head.

Instantly, I jumped to my feet and lunged at Darby, slashing at his heavy jaw with sizzling rights and lefts, backing him up. Twelve years of rage surged through my veins. I split his forehead over one eye and tore a rip in the skin beneath the other. I threw a wicked left cross that grazed his jaw. He drove a straight right into my chin.

Stars flashed in my eyes, and my ears rang like Christmas bells.

He kicked at me, but I grabbed his boot and shoved him backward, sending him tumbling over the barrel of pickles, spilling them all over the floor.

With a guttural growl, he lumbered to his feet and, lowering his head, charged. I sidestepped and threw a straight right into the side of his head as he stumbled past. With a roar like a wounded animal, he spun and charged again, blood dripping from his face.

This time, he guessed which way I would move and drove his head into my belly, knocking me back on a counter and sending me tumbling backward over it. "Now, I got you," he said through clenched teeth, placing a hand on the counter and vaulting over it.

Still on my back, I aimed both heels at his knees,

kicking his legs from under him and sending him to
the floor. He fell on my feet and grabbed at them. I
jerked a foot loose and kicked him in the face.

Screaming in pain, he stumbled to his feet.

I jumped to my feet first. I wiped the blood from
my eyes and measured his jaw. Using every pound of
my body, I swung a half-uppercut, half-cross, catching
him on his rock-like jaw. He took a step back, wiped
the blood from his eyes, and stepped forward behind
a vicious right.

I blocked the right and caught him on the chin with
a left.

And then we stood toe-to-toe, slugging it out. My
breath came in gasps, burning my lungs. My arms felt
like lead weights, but I clenched my teeth and kept
punching, slamming my fists into his cast-iron belly
and granite jaw.

Blood filled my eyes. I blinked to clear them, and
suddenly, Darby was gone.

I looked down, and he lay on the floor at my feet,
moaning.

Savagely, I jerked him to his feet and slammed him
against the wall. "It's time, Darby. Who was the fifth
man? Tell me, and I won't kill you."

He tried to sneer, but his split and swollen lips could
not curl. He spit on the floor at my feet.

Cold resolution flowed through my body. I slid the
double-edged knife from my boot. I shoved Darby
down on the counter and ripped his shirt open. "Talk,
or I swear on my dead brother's grave, I'll open you

like a hog." I pressed the tip of the knife into the middle of his breastbone, penetrating the skin and drawing a bubble of blood around the tip. "From chest to groin, Darby."

He tried to sneer, but I saw the fear come to life in his dark eyes. I drew the knife half an inch down his chest, opening the skin. "One more chance, and I'll leave you here for the vermin and scavengers."

Behind me, a feminine voice gasped. "Jed! No."

I kept my eyes on Darby. "Get out of here, Mary Catherine. Don't interfere."

Arch spoke up. "Listen, Jed. I've got something to tell you. You got to listen."

"No!" I shouted, glaring down at Darby. "This is my business. Get her out of here." I leaned over the prone man.

Darby's eyes grew wide when he read the determination in mine. "No. Don't. Don't gut me. I'll tell you. I'll tell you. I don't know where he is now. Honest. He was just a kid."

I hissed. "His name, Darby. What was his name?"

His voice trembling, he gasped out, "Arch Hopkins."

Behind me, Mary Catherine gasped.

I stared at Darby in disbelief. "Don't lie to me."

"I ain't lying. There was five of us. The kid joined up just before we hit you and your brother. Wet-nosed kid trying to be a man. That was his name. I swear to heaven, that was his name. Arch Hopkins. He didn't even know what we was up to."

In a daze, I released my grip on his shirt. Woodenly, I turned to face Arch and Mary Catherine. From the look on their faces, I knew Darby had told me the truth. Arch was the fifth man. I gripped the knife in my hand. I tried to sort out my feelings, but my thoughts were more tangled than a runaway steer in a barbed wire fence.

Arch took a step toward me. "Jed! I tried to tell you. I—"

I couldn't look at him. I brushed past, ignoring Mary Catherine's outstretched hand. Arch. The fifth man. The one I had sworn to kill.

As I reached the door, Arch shouted, "Darby! No!"

I spun as Darby leveled the Henry at me.

The rifle boomed just as Arch leaped in front of it.

In a blur, I whipped the knife over my head and hurled it at Darby.

He gasped and looked with stunned disbelief at the knife handle protruding from his chest, just over his heart. He grasped the handle with both hands and tried to pull it out, but all his strength was draining from his body.

He gave a pitiful moan as his legs grew rubbery and he crumpled to the floor.

"Arch!" Mary Catherine screamed and rushed to her brother's side. She knelt by him, imploring him to speak to her, but his eyes remained closed. She looked around at me, her eyes pleading. "Jed. Please, help him. Please."

I felt all empty inside, like everything had been ripped out.

At my side, Cyrus laid his hand on my arm. I looked down at him, and saw the same pleading for help in his eyes.

I tried to push the emotion churning inside from my thoughts and focus on the present. "Get some fresh water," I told Cyrus as I crossed the room to Arch.

The storeowner stood wide-eyed behind the counter. "You," I said, "get over here and help me get him on the counter." With a sweep of my arm, I brushed the shirts and jeans from the counter.

We lifted Arch onto the counter, and I unfastened his shirt. The slug had struck his chest above the heart, but one of the conchos had deflected it upward, where it exited beneath his shoulder. He was bleeding pro-fusely.

"First thing," I muttered, "we've got to stop the bleeding."

I packed clean pads on both sides of the wound, but within minutes they were soaked.

Mary Catherine looked up at me, her tear-filled eyes red and her brow knit in fear. "Is he—is he going to die?"

Despite the chill in the air, sweat ran down my fore-head and stung my eyes as I worked desperately to staunch the flow of blood.

Arch seemed to be growing weaker.

"Jed! Look."

I looked around to see Horse In Water and his father, Tall Cougar, in the doorway. Behind them, another half dozen Chickasaw warriors sat astride their ponies.

Regal in stature and demeanor, Tall Cougar crossed the room to Arch. He inspected the wound, then looked around at me. "White man bad." He touched his finger to my chest. "You friend. We help." He pointed east. "We take to camp. Make better."

It was well after sundown by the time we reached the camp, which consisted of several lodges of pine logs. The warriors carefully carried Arch into a lodge and laid him on the floor beside the fire.

We joined him, looking on as the old medicine man applied various poultices and plasters, all of which carried a stench that made a hog pen seem like a field of roses. To my surprise and relief, Arch seemed to rest easier.

The Indian women brought us a meal of porridge and venison. While we ate, Tall Cougar related how he had ordered his scouts to keep us in their sight and out of danger.

Cyrus looked up at me, a smug grin on his face. "See, it wasn't my imagination."

I grinned at him. "No, sir, I don't reckon it was."

While we were together, Mary Catherine seemed distant, though from time to time I'd catch her looking at me.

All that had happened in the last few hours, all I had learned, left me confused. I didn't know how I felt about Arch, about Mary Catherine, about the vow I had taken twelve years earlier.

The old medicine man remained at Arch's side, motionless.

Later, after Cyrus had dropped off to sleep, I sat staring into the fire, hoping to draw some wisdom from the flickering, soothing flames.

A soft voice came from the shadows beyond the fire. "Can't sleep?" It was Mary Catherine.

I paused before answering. "No," was all I said. I didn't feel like talking, not to her, not to anyone.

She sat up and pulled the blanket around her shoulders. "You know, Jed, Arch wanted to tell you."

I snapped at her. "Then maybe he should have. If he wanted to tell me so bad, he should have."

Mary Catherine smiled tolerantly. "Yes, he should have. From the time back at the ranch when you told us what happened, he guessed. He knew for sure when you two talked later that night. He was just an irresponsible, wild kid. That was the only thing he ever did wrong in his life, and it has haunted him all these years, even if he wasn't the one who pulled the trigger. Just being with that gang of scum on that day has scarred him for life."

Arch stirred.

The old man laid his hand on Arch's chest, then peeked under the poultice. He patted it back in place and turned his rheumy eyes to me. He nodded once, then slowly rose to his feet and left the lodge.

I nodded to Mary Catherine. "Arch'll be fine."

"Thank you," she whispered. "You saved his life."

"Not me. It was the Chickasaw."

"But they wouldn't have helped if you hadn't taken care of Horse in Water."

When I frowned at her, she explained. "Cyrus told me." She paused, then said, "That boy thinks the world of you, Jed."

For a moment, I remained silent. "Well, I hope he learns soon that things aren't always what they seem." Taking a deep breath, I rose and stepped outside into the bracing chill of the night.

Overhead, glittering stars filled the heavens, in some places as thick as the vast meadows of bluebonnets carpeting the Texas prairies.

Tall Cougar appeared at my side. He looked at the lodge.

I nodded. "He'll be okay." I offered him my hand. "Thank you."

"You and your friends will stay until he can ride."

For several moments, I considered his offer, but so much had happened, so much I couldn't get straight in my head. "Much obliged, but I reckon I'll ride on out. The others can stay, but it's time for me to go."

Somberly, he nodded. "I will be sad when you leave, but you are always welcome here."

I studied the lodge in which Arch lay. Mary Catherine's words played over in my head. Maybe, in a way, I did save Arch's life, but twice he'd saved mine. The first was during the attack on the Comanche camp, and the second was today with Darby.

Maybe that was my payback.

A sudden peacefulness came over me. I looked up at the stars again. "You know, Ma, I saved him. He saved me. Maybe that's another way to look at an eye for an eye. Or maybe like Langdon Beauchamp said, 'if thine eye offend thee, pluck it out.' "

I wasn't smart enough to know which one was right. Maybe they both were. Maybe neither was. But, I finally had it straight in my own mind.

For a moment I studied the stars. One shot across the heaven. "If that's you, Ma, rest easy. I kept my promise."

Chapter Nineteen

Arch was awake the next morning. "I wanted to tell you, Jed. I—I just didn't know how."

I glanced at Mary Catherine and grinned at Arch. "It was a long time ago. You were a kid, not much older than Cyrus here. Let it go. I have."

Mary Catherine's eyes grew wide.

Arch stared hard at me. "Have you, Jed? Have you really?"

To my surprise, the answer came unhesitatingly to my lips. "Yes."

Mary Catherine cleared her throat.

Arch glanced at her, then looked up at me. "Jed, I'd be mighty pleased if you'd come back to the ranch with us. It would be a fine place for Cyrus, and maybe it would somehow make up for the hurt I did to you."

I reached for my hat. "I'm much obliged, but I'm

182

riding on. I do appreciate you taking Cyrus. A younger needs a solid foundation. He don't need to be traipsing the country, never putting down roots. Why—"

Cyrus interrupted me. "I ain't going with them if you don't."

I looked around at him, taken aback by his defiance. "Don't talk to me like that, boy. You'll do what I say. You need a home, not some will-o'the-wisp life."

He shook his head. "I'll follow you. Just like last time."

A soft but determined feminine voice chimed in. "I'll follow you too."

Well, sir, I felt like a pole-axed steer when those words hit me. I was so flustered, I couldn't think. Finally, I managed to choke out, "But what about Red?"

She rose to her feet and gave her head a defiant toss. "What about Red?"

"Well, I sorta figured that you and him—"

Mary Catherine shook her head sharply. "That's your problem, Jed Walker. You think too much at times. You think you can tell me who I should be interested in?"

I took a step backward, flustered by the surprising ire in her voice. "Well. No. Not really. I reckon not."

Arch just grinned.

She gave a sharp nod. "Good, because from the first time I saw you, I knew you and me would someday get married."

The grin on Cyrus's face was wider than the Sabine River, just about a match for the one Arch wore.

All I could do was stare at Mary Catherine. She took a step forward. "Well, Jed Walker. Are you going to kiss me, or do I have to do all the work?"

Well, sir, I kissed her, and I plumb well kissed her good.